MY MAN JEEVES

MY MAN JEEVES

BY
P. G. WODEHOUSE

ISBN: 978-93-5128-387-4(HB)

First Published in 1919
Indian Reprint in 2017

Published by

Kalpaz Publications
C-30, Satyawati Nagar,
Delhi – 110052
E-mail: kalpaz@hotmail.com
Website: kalpazpublications.com
Ph.: +91-9212142040

Cataloging in Publication Data—DK

Courtesy: D.K. Agencies (P) Ltd. <docinfo@dkagencies.com>

Wodehouse, P. G. (Pelham Grenville), 1881-1975, **author.**

My man Jeeves / by P.G. Wodehouse.
pages cm
Novel.

"First published in 1919"

ISBN 9789351283874 (HB)

1. Wooster, Bertie (Fictitious character)—Fiction. 2. Jeeves (Fictitious character)—Fiction. 3. Single men—Fiction. 4. Valets—Fiction. 5. Humorous stories, English. I. Title.

LCC PR6045.O53M96 2017 | DDC 823.914 23

CONTENTS

CHAPTER — PAGES

LEAVE IT TO JEEVES 7

JEEVES AND THE UNBIDDEN GUEST 22

JEEVES AND THE HARD-BOILED EGG 38

ABSENT TREATMENT 54

HELPING FREDDIE 65

RALLYING ROUND OLD GEORGE 76

DOING CLARENCE A BIT OF GOOD 90

THE AUNT AND THE SLUGGARD 103

CHAPTER - 1

LEAVE IT TO JEEVES

Jeeves—my man, you know—is really a most extraordinary chap. So capable. Honestly, I shouldn't know what to do without him. On broader lines he's like those chappies who sit peering sadly over the marble battlements at the Pennsylvania Station in the place marked "Inquiries." You know the Johnnies I mean. You go up to them and say: "When's the next train for Melonsquashville, Tennessee?" and they reply, without stopping to think, "Two-forty-three, track ten, change at San Francisco." And they're right every time. Well, Jeeves gives you just the same impression of omniscience.

As an instance of what I mean, I remember meeting Monty Byng in Bond Street one morning, looking the last word in a grey check suit, and I felt I should never be happy till I had one like it. I dug the address of the tailors out of him, and had them working on the thing inside the hour.

"Jeeves," I said that evening. "I'm getting a check suit like that one of Mr. Byng's."

"Injudicious, sir," he said firmly. "It will not become you."

"What absolute rot! It's the soundest thing I've struck for years."

"Unsuitable for you, sir."

Well, the long and the short of it was that the confounded thing came home, and I put it on, and when I caught sight of myself in the glass I nearly swooned. Jeeves was perfectly right. I looked a cross between a music-hall comedian and a cheap bookie. Yet Monty had looked fine in absolutely the same stuff. These things are just Life's mysteries, and that's all there is to it.

But it isn't only that Jeeves's judgment about clothes is infallible, though, of course, that's really the main thing. The man knows everything. There was the matter of that tip on the "Lincolnshire." I forget now how I got it, but it had the aspect of being the real, red-hot tabasco.

"Jeeves," I said, for I'm fond of the man, and like to do him a good turn when I can, "if you want to make a bit of money have something on Wonderchild for the 'Lincolnshire.'"

He shook his head.

"I'd rather not, sir."

"But it's the straight goods. I'm going to put my shirt on him."

"I do not recommend it, sir. The animal is not intended to win. Second place is what the stable is after."

Perfect piffle, I thought, of course. How the deuce could Jeeves know anything about it? Still, you know what happened. Wonderchild led till he was breathing on the wire, and then Banana Fritter came along and nosed him out. I went straight home and rang for Jeeves.

"After this," I said, "not another step for me without your advice. From now on consider yourself the brains of the establishment."

"Very good, sir. I shall endeavour to give satisfaction."

And he has, by Jove! I'm a bit short on brain myself; the old bean would appear to have been constructed more for ornament than for use, don't you know; but give me five minutes to talk the thing over with Jeeves, and I'm game to advise any one about anything. And that's why, when Bruce Corcoran came to me with his troubles, my first act was to ring the bell and put it up to the lad with the bulging forehead.

"Leave it to Jeeves," I said.

I first got to know Corky when I came to New York. He was a pal of my cousin Gussie, who was in with a lot of people down Washington Square way. I don't know if I ever told you about it, but the reason why I left England was because I was sent over by my Aunt Agatha to try to stop young Gussie marrying a girl on the vaudeville stage, and I got the whole thing so mixed up that I decided that it would be a sound scheme for me to stop on in America for a bit instead of going back and having long cosy chats about the thing with aunt. So I sent Jeeves out to find a decent apartment, and settled down for a bit of exile. I'm bound to say that New York's a topping place to be exiled in. Everybody was awfully good to me, and there seemed to be plenty of things going on, and I'm a wealthy bird, so everything was fine. Chappies introduced me to other chappies, and so on and so forth, and it wasn't long before I knew squads of the right sort, some who rolled in dollars in houses up by the Park, and others who lived with the gas turned down mostly around Washington Square—artists and writers and so forth. Brainy coves.

Corky was one of the artists. A portrait-painter, he called himself, but he hadn't painted any portraits. He was sitting on the side-lines with a blanket over his shoulders, waiting for a chance to get into the game. You see, the catch about portrait-painting—I've looked into the thing a bit—is that you can't start painting portraits till people come along and ask you to, and they won't come and ask you to until you've painted a lot first. This makes it kind of difficult for a chappie. Corky managed to get along by drawing an occasional picture for the comic papers—he had rather a gift for funny stuff when he got a good idea—and doing bedsteads and chairs and things for the advertisements. His principal source of income, however, was derived from biting the ear of a rich uncle—one Alexander Worple, who was in the jute business. I'm a bit foggy as to what jute is, but it's apparently something the populace is pretty keen on, for Mr. Worple had made quite an indecently large stack out of it.

Now, a great many fellows think that having a rich uncle is a pretty soft snap: but, according to Corky, such is not the case. Corky's uncle was a robust sort of cove, who looked like living for ever. He was fifty-one, and it seemed as if he might go to par. It was not this, however, that distressed poor old Corky, for he was not bigoted and had no objection to the man going on living. What Corky kicked at was the way the above Worple used to harry him.

Corky's uncle, you see, didn't want him to be an artist. He didn't think he had any talent in that direction. He was always urging him to chuck Art and go into the jute business and start at the bottom and work his way up. Jute had apparently become a sort of obsession with him. He seemed to attach almost a spiritual importance to it. And what Corky said was that, while he didn't know what they did at the bottom of the jute business, instinct told him that it was something too beastly for words. Corky, moreover, believed in his future as an artist. Some day, he said, he was going to make a hit. Meanwhile, by using the utmost tact and persuasiveness, he was inducing his uncle to cough up very grudgingly a small quarterly allowance.

He wouldn't have got this if his uncle hadn't had a hobby. Mr. Worple was peculiar in this respect. As a rule, from what I've observed, the American captain of industry doesn't do anything out of business hours. When he has put the cat out and locked up the office for the night, he just relapses into a state of coma from which he emerges only to start being a captain of industry again. But Mr. Worple in his spare time was what is known as an ornithologist. He had written a book called *American Birds*, and was writing another, to be called *More American Birds*. When he had finished that, the presumption was that he would begin a third, and keep on till the supply of American birds gave out. Corky used to go to him about once every three months and let him talk about American birds. Apparently you could do what you liked with old Worple if you gave him his head first on his pet subject, so these little chats used to make Corky's allowance all right for the time being. But it was pretty rotten for the poor chap. There was the frightful suspense, you see, and, apart from that, birds, except when broiled and in the society of a cold bottle, bored him stiff.

To complete the character-study of Mr. Worple, he was a man of extremely uncertain temper, and his general tendency was to think that Corky was a poor chump and that whatever step he took in any direction on his own account, was just another proof of his innate idiocy. I should imagine Jeeves feels very much the same about me.

So when Corky trickled into my apartment one afternoon, shooing a girl in front of him, and said, "Bertie, I want you to meet my fiancée, Miss Singer," the aspect of the matter which hit me first was precisely the one which he had come to consult me about. The very first words I spoke were, "Corky, how about your uncle?"

The poor chap gave one of those mirthless laughs. He was looking anxious and worried, like a man who has done the murder all right but can't think what the deuce to do with the body.

"We're so scared, Mr. Wooster," said the girl. "We were hoping that you might suggest a way of breaking it to him."

Muriel Singer was one of those very quiet, appealing girls who have a way of looking at you with their big eyes as if they thought you were the greatest thing on earth and wondered that you hadn't got on to it yet yourself. She sat there in a sort of shrinking way, looking at me as if she were saying to herself, "Oh, I do hope this great strong man isn't going to hurt me." She gave a fellow a protective kind of feeling, made him want to stroke her hand and say, "There, there, little one!" or words to that effect. She made me feel that there was nothing I wouldn't do for her. She was rather like one of those innocent-tasting American drinks which creep imperceptibly into your system so that, before you know what you're doing, you're starting out to reform the world by force if necessary and pausing on your way to tell the large man in the corner that, if he looks at you like that, you will knock his head off. What I mean is, she made me feel alert and dashing, like a jolly old knight-errant or something of that kind. I felt that I was with her in this thing to the limit.

"I don't see why your uncle shouldn't be most awfully bucked," I said to Corky. "He will think Miss Singer the ideal wife for you."

Corky declined to cheer up.

"You don't know him. Even if he did like Muriel he wouldn't admit it. That's the sort of pig-headed guy he is. It would be a matter of principle with him to kick. All he would consider would be that I had gone and taken an important step without asking his advice, and he would raise Cain automatically. He's always done it."

I strained the old bean to meet this emergency.

"You want to work it so that he makes Miss Singer's acquaintance without knowing that you know her. Then you come along——"

"But how can I work it that way?"

I saw his point. That was the catch.

"There's only one thing to do," I said.

"What's that?"

"Leave it to Jeeves."

And I rang the bell.

"Sir?" said Jeeves, kind of manifesting himself. One of the rummy things about Jeeves is that, unless you watch like a hawk, you very seldom see him come into a room. He's like one of those weird chappies in India who dissolve themselves into thin air and nip through space in a sort of disembodied way and assemble the parts again just where they want them. I've got a cousin who's what they call a Theosophist, and he says he's often nearly worked the thing himself, but couldn't quite bring it off, probably owing to having fed in his boyhood on the flesh of animals slain in anger and pie.

The moment I saw the man standing there, registering respectful attention, a weight seemed to roll off my mind. I felt like a lost child who spots his father in the offing. There was something about him that gave me confidence.

Jeeves is a tallish man, with one of those dark, shrewd faces. His eye gleams with the light of pure intelligence.

"Jeeves, we want your advice."

"Very good, sir."

I boiled down Corky's painful case into a few well-chosen words.

"So you see what it amount to, Jeeves. We want you to suggest some way by which Mr. Worple can make Miss Singer's acquaintance without getting on to the fact that Mr. Corcoran already knows her. Understand?"

"Perfectly, sir."

"Well, try to think of something."

"I have thought of something already, sir."

"You have!"

"The scheme I would suggest cannot fail of success, but it has what may seem to you a drawback, sir, in that it requires a certain financial outlay."

"He means," I translated to Corky, "that he has got a pippin of an idea, but it's going to cost a bit."

Naturally the poor chap's face dropped, for this seemed to dish the whole thing. But I was still under the influence of the girl's melting gaze, and I saw that this was where I started in as a knight-errant.

"You can count on me for all that sort of thing, Corky," I said. "Only too glad. Carry on, Jeeves."

"I would suggest, sir, that Mr. Corcoran take advantage of Mr. Worple's attachment to ornithology."

"How on earth did you know that he was fond of birds?"

"It is the way these New York apartments are constructed, sir. Quite unlike our London houses. The partitions between the rooms are of the flimsiest nature. With no wish to overhear, I have sometimes heard Mr. Corcoran expressing himself with a generous strength on the subject I have mentioned."

"Oh! Well?"

"Why should not the young lady write a small volume, to be entitled—let us say—*The Children's Book of American Birds*, and dedicate it to Mr. Worple! A limited edition could be published at your expense, sir, and a great deal of the book would, of course, be given over to eulogistic remarks concerning Mr. Worple's own larger treatise on the same subject. I should recommend the dispatching of a presentation copy to Mr. Worple, immediately on publication, accompanied by a letter in which the young lady asks to be allowed to make the acquaintance of one to whom she owes so much. This would, I fancy, produce the desired result, but as I say, the expense involved would be considerable."

I felt like the proprietor of a performing dog on the vaudeville stage when the tyke has just pulled off his trick without a hitch. I had betted on Jeeves all along, and I had known that he wouldn't let me down. It beats me sometimes why a man with his genius is satisfied to hang around pressing my clothes and what-not. If I had half Jeeves's brain, I should have a stab at being Prime Minister or something.

"Jeeves," I said, "that is absolutely ripping! One of your very best efforts."

"Thank you, sir."

The girl made an objection.

"But I'm sure I couldn't write a book about anything. I can't even write good letters."

"Muriel's talents," said Corky, with a little cough "lie more in the direction of the drama, Bertie. I didn't mention it before, but one of our reasons for being a trifle nervous as to how Uncle Alexander will receive the news is that Muriel is in the chorus of that show *Choose your Exit* at the Manhattan. It's absurdly unreasonable, but we both feel that that fact might increase Uncle Alexander's natural tendency to kick like a steer."

I saw what he meant. Goodness knows there was fuss enough in our family when I tried to marry into musical comedy a few years ago. And the recollection of my Aunt Agatha's attitude in the matter of Gussie and the vaudeville girl was still fresh in my mind. I don't know why it is—one of these psychology sharps could explain it, I suppose—but uncles and aunts, as a class, are always dead against the drama, legitimate or otherwise. They don't seem able to stick it at any price.

But Jeeves had a solution, of course.

"I fancy it would be a simple matter, sir, to find some impecunious author who would be glad to do the actual composition of the volume for a small fee. It is only necessary that the young lady's name should appear on the title page."

"That's true," said Corky. "Sam Patterson would do it for a hundred dollars. He writes a novelette, three short stories, and ten thousand words of a serial for one of the all-fiction magazines under different names every month. A little thing like this would be nothing to him. I'll get after him right away."

"Fine!"

"Will that be all, sir?" said Jeeves. "Very good, sir. Thank you, sir."

I always used to think that publishers had to be devilish intelligent fellows, loaded down with the grey matter; but I've got their number now. All a publisher has to do is to write cheques at intervals, while a lot of deserving and industrious chappies rally round and do the real work. I know, because I've been one myself. I simply sat tight in the old apartment with a fountain-pen, and in due season a topping, shiny book came along.

I happened to be down at Corky's place when the first copies of *The Children's Book of American Birds* bobbed up. Muriel Singer was there, and we were talking of things in general when there was a bang at the door and the parcel was delivered.

It was certainly some book. It had a red cover with a fowl of some species on it, and underneath the girl's name in gold letters. I opened a copy at random.

"Often of a spring morning," it said at the top of page twenty-one, "as you wander through the fields, you will hear the sweet-toned, carelessly flowing warble of the purple finch linnet. When you are older you must read all about him in Mr. Alexander Worple's wonderful book—*American Birds*."

You see. A boost for the uncle right away. And only a few pages later there he was in the limelight again in connection with the yellow-billed cuckoo. It was great stuff. The more I read, the more I admired the chap who had written it and Jeeves's genius in putting us on to the wheeze. I didn't see how the uncle could fail to drop. You can't call a chap the world's greatest authority on the yellow-billed cuckoo without rousing a certain disposition towards chumminess in him.

"It's a cert!" I said.

"An absolute cinch!" said Corky.

And a day or two later he meandered up the Avenue to my apartment to tell me that all was well. The uncle had written Muriel a letter so dripping with the milk of human kindness that if he hadn't known Mr. Worple's handwriting Corky would have refused to believe him the author of it. Any time it suited Miss Singer to call, said the uncle, he would be delighted to make her acquaintance.

Shortly after this I had to go out of town. Divers sound sportsmen had invited me to pay visits to their country places, and it wasn't for several months that I settled down in the city again. I had been wondering a lot, of course, about Corky, whether it all turned out right, and so forth, and my first evening in New York, happening to pop into a quiet sort of little restaurant which I go to when I don't feel inclined for the bright lights, I found Muriel Singer there, sitting by herself at a table near the door. Corky, I took it, was out telephoning. I went up and passed the time of day.

"Well, well, well, what?" I said.

"Why, Mr. Wooster! How do you do?"

"Corky around?"

"I beg your pardon?"

"You're waiting for Corky, aren't you?"

"Oh, I didn't understand. No, I'm not waiting for him."

It seemed to me that there was a sort of something in her voice, a kind of thingummy, you know.

"I say, you haven't had a row with Corky, have you?"

"A row?"

"A spat, don't you know—little misunderstanding—faults on both sides—er—and all that sort of thing."

"Why, whatever makes you think that?"

"Oh, well, as it were, what? What I mean is—I thought you usually dined with him before you went to the theatre."

"I've left the stage now."

Suddenly the whole thing dawned on me. I had forgotten what a long time I had been away.

"Why, of course, I see now! You're married!"

"Yes."

"How perfectly topping! I wish you all kinds of happiness."

"Thank you, so much. Oh Alexander," she said, looking past me, "this is a friend of mine—Mr. Wooster."

I spun round. A chappie with a lot of stiff grey hair and a red sort of healthy face was standing there. Rather a formidable Johnnie, he looked, though quite peaceful at the moment.

"I want you to meet my husband, Mr. Wooster. Mr. Wooster is a friend of Bruce's, Alexander."

The old boy grasped my hand warmly, and that was all that kept me from hitting the floor in a heap. The place was rocking. Absolutely.

"So you know my nephew, Mr. Wooster," I heard him say. "I wish you would try to knock a little sense into him and make him quit this playing at painting. But I have an idea that he is steadying down. I noticed it first that night he came to dinner with us, my dear, to be introduced to you. He seemed altogether quieter and more serious. Something seemed to have sobered him. Perhaps you will give us the pleasure of your company at dinner to-night, Mr. Wooster? Or have you dined?"

I said I had. What I needed then was air, not dinner. I felt that I wanted to get into the open and think this thing out.

When I reached my apartment I heard Jeeves moving about in his lair. I called him.

"Jeeves," I said, "now is the time for all good men to come to the aid of the party. A stiff b.-and-s. first of all, and then I've a bit of news for you."

He came back with a tray and a long glass.

"Better have one yourself, Jeeves. You'll need it."

"Later on, perhaps, thank you, sir."

"All right. Please yourself. But you're going to get a shock. You remember my friend, Mr. Corcoran?"

"Yes, sir."

"And the girl who was to slide gracefully into his uncle's esteem by writing the book on birds?"

"Perfectly, sir."

"Well, she's slid. She's married the uncle."

He took it without blinking. You can't rattle Jeeves.

"That was always a development to be feared, sir."

"You don't mean to tell me that you were expecting it?"

"It crossed my mind as a possibility."

"Did it, by Jove! Well, I think, you might have warned us!"

"I hardly liked to take the liberty, sir."

Of course, as I saw after I had had a bite to eat and was in a calmer frame of mind, what had happened wasn't my fault, if you come down to it. I couldn't be expected to foresee that the scheme, in itself a cracker-jack, would skid into the ditch as it had done; but all the same I'm bound to admit that I didn't relish the idea of meeting Corky again until time, the great healer, had been able to get in a bit of soothing work. I cut Washington Square out absolutely for the next few months. I gave it the complete miss-in-baulk. And then, just when I was beginning to think I might safely pop down in that direction and gather up the dropped threads, so to speak, time, instead of working the healing wheeze, went and pulled the most awful bone and put the lid on it. Opening the paper one morning, I read that Mrs. Alexander Worple had presented her husband with a son and heir.

I was so darned sorry for poor old Corky that I hadn't the heart to touch my breakfast. I told Jeeves to drink it himself. I was bowled over. Absolutely. It was the limit.

I hardly knew what to do. I wanted, of course, to rush down to Washington Square and grip the poor blighter silently by the hand; and then, thinking it over, I hadn't the nerve. Absent treatment seemed the touch. I gave it him in waves.

But after a month or so I began to hesitate again. It struck me that it was playing it a bit low-down on the poor chap, avoiding him like this just when he probably wanted his pals to surge round him most. I pictured him sitting in his lonely studio with no company but his bitter thoughts, and the pathos of it got me to such an extent that I bounded straight into a taxi and told the driver to go all out for the studio.

I rushed in, and there was Corky, hunched up at the easel, painting away, while on the model throne sat a severe-looking female of middle age, holding a baby.

A fellow has to be ready for that sort of thing.

"Oh, ah!" I said, and started to back out.

Corky looked over his shoulder.

"Halloa, Bertie. Don't go. We're just finishing for the day. That will be all this afternoon," he said to the nurse, who got up with the baby and decanted it into a perambulator which was standing in the fairway.

"At the same hour to-morrow, Mr. Corcoran?"

"Yes, please."

"Good afternoon."

"Good afternoon."

Corky stood there, looking at the door, and then he turned to me and began to get it off his chest. Fortunately, he seemed to take it for granted that I knew all about what had happened, so it wasn't as awkward as it might have been.

"It's my uncle's idea," he said. "Muriel doesn't know about it yet. The portrait's to be a surprise for her on her birthday. The nurse takes the kid out ostensibly to get a breather, and they beat it down here. If you want an instance of the irony of fate, Bertie, get acquainted with this. Here's the first commission I have ever had to paint a portrait, and the sitter is that human poached egg that has butted in and bounced me out of my inheritance. Can you beat it! I call it rubbing the thing in to expect me to spend my afternoons gazing into the ugly face of a little brat who to all intents and purposes has hit me behind the ear with a blackjack and swiped all I possess. I can't refuse to paint the portrait because if I did my uncle would stop my allowance; yet every time I look up and catch that kid's vacant eye, I suffer agonies. I tell you, Bertie, sometimes when he gives me a patronizing glance and then turns away and is sick, as if it revolted him to look at me, I come within an ace of occupying the entire front page of the evening papers as the latest murder sensation. There are moments when I can almost see the headlines: 'Promising Young Artist Beans Baby With Axe.'"

I patted his shoulder silently. My sympathy for the poor old scout was too deep for words.

I kept away from the studio for some time after that, because it didn't seem right to me to intrude on the poor chappie's sorrow. Besides, I'm bound to say that nurse intimidated me. She reminded me so infernally of Aunt Agatha. She was the same gimlet-eyed type.

But one afternoon Corky called me on the 'phone.

"Bertie."

"Halloa?"

"Are you doing anything this afternoon?"

"Nothing special."

"You couldn't come down here, could you?"

"What's the trouble? Anything up?"

"I've finished the portrait."

"Good boy! Stout work!"

"Yes." His voice sounded rather doubtful. "The fact is, Bertie, it doesn't look quite right to me. There's something about it—My uncle's coming in half an hour to inspect it, and—I don't know why it is, but I kind of feel I'd like your moral support!"

I began to see that I was letting myself in for something. The sympathetic co-operation of Jeeves seemed to me to be indicated.

"You think he'll cut up rough?"

"He may."

I threw my mind back to the red-faced chappie I had met at the restaurant, and tried to picture him cutting up rough. It was only too easy. I spoke to Corky firmly on the telephone.

"I'll come," I said.

"Good!"

"But only if I may bring Jeeves!"

"Why Jeeves? What's Jeeves got to do with it? Who wants Jeeves? Jeeves is the fool who suggested the scheme that has led——"

"Listen, Corky, old top! If you think I am going to face that uncle of yours without Jeeves's support, you're mistaken. I'd sooner go into a den of wild beasts and bite a lion on the back of the neck."

"Oh, all right," said Corky. Not cordially, but he said it; so I rang for Jeeves, and explained the situation.

"Very good, sir," said Jeeves.

That's the sort of chap he is. You can't rattle him.

We found Corky near the door, looking at the picture, with one hand up in a defensive sort of way, as if he thought it might swing on him.

"Stand right where you are, Bertie," he said, without moving. "Now, tell me honestly, how does it strike you?"

The light from the big window fell right on the picture. I took a good look at it. Then I shifted a bit nearer and took another look. Then I went back to where I had been at first, because it hadn't seemed quite so bad from there.

"Well?" said Corky, anxiously.

I hesitated a bit.

"Of course, old man, I only saw the kid once, and then only for a moment, but—but it *was* an ugly sort of kid, wasn't it, if I remember rightly?"

"As ugly as that?"

I looked again, and honesty compelled me to be frank.

"I don't see how it could have been, old chap."

Poor old Corky ran his fingers through his hair in a temperamental sort of way. He groaned.

"You're right quite, Bertie. Something's gone wrong with the darned thing. My private impression is that, without knowing it, I've worked that stunt that Sargent and those fellows pull—painting the soul of the sitter. I've got through the mere outward appearance, and have put the child's soul on canvas."

"But could a child of that age have a soul like that? I don't see how he could have managed it in the time. What do you think, Jeeves?"

"I doubt it, sir."

"It—it sorts of leers at you, doesn't it?"

"You've noticed that, too?" said Corky.

"I don't see how one could help noticing."

"All I tried to do was to give the little brute a cheerful expression. But, as it worked out, he looks positively dissipated."

"Just what I was going to suggest, old man. He looks as if he were in the middle of a colossal spree, and enjoying every minute of it. Don't you think so, Jeeves?"

"He has a decidedly inebriated air, sir."

Corky was starting to say something when the door opened, and the uncle came in.

For about three seconds all was joy, jollity, and goodwill. The old boy shook hands with me, slapped Corky on the back, said that he didn't think he had ever seen such a fine day, and whacked his leg with his stick. Jeeves had projected himself into the background, and he didn't notice him.

"Well, Bruce, my boy; so the portrait is really finished, is it—really finished? Well, bring it out. Let's have a look at it. This will be a wonderful surprise for your aunt. Where is it? Let's——"

And then he got it—suddenly, when he wasn't set for the punch; and he rocked back on his heels.

"Oosh!" he exclaimed. And for perhaps a minute there was one of the scaliest silences I've ever run up against.

"Is this a practical joke?" he said at last, in a way that set about sixteen draughts cutting through the room at once.

I thought it was up to me to rally round old Corky.

"You want to stand a bit farther away from it," I said.

"You're perfectly right!" he snorted. "I do! I want to stand so far away from it that I can't see the thing with a telescope!" He turned on Corky like an untamed tiger of the jungle who has just located a chunk of meat. "And this—this—is what you have been wasting your time and my money for all these years! A painter! I wouldn't let you paint a house of mine! I gave you this commission, thinking that you were a competent worker, and this—this—this extract from a comic coloured supplement is the result!" He swung towards the door, lashing his tail and growling to himself. "This ends it! If you wish to continue this foolery of pretending to be an artist because you want an excuse for idleness, please yourself. But let me tell you this. Unless you report at my office on Monday morning, prepared to abandon all this idiocy and start in at the bottom of the business to work your way up, as you should have done half a dozen years ago, not another cent—not another cent—not another—Boosh!"

Then the door closed, and he was no longer with us. And I crawled out of the bombproof shelter.

"Corky, old top!" I whispered faintly.

Corky was standing staring at the picture. His face was set. There was a hunted look in his eye.

"Well, that finishes it!" he muttered brokenly.

"What are you going to do?"

"Do? What can I do? I can't stick on here if he cuts off supplies. You heard what he said. I shall have to go to the office on Monday."

I couldn't think of a thing to say. I knew exactly how he felt about the office. I don't know when I've been so infernally uncomfortable. It was like hanging round trying to make conversation to a pal who's just been sentenced to twenty years in quod.

And then a soothing voice broke the silence.

"If I might make a suggestion, sir!"

It was Jeeves. He had slid from the shadows and was gazing gravely at the picture. Upon my word, I can't give you a better idea of the shattering effect of Corky's uncle Alexander when in action than by saying that he had absolutely made me forget for the moment that Jeeves was there.

"I wonder if I have ever happened to mention to you, sir, a Mr. Digby Thistleton, with whom I was once in service? Perhaps you have met him? He was a financier. He is now Lord Bridgnorth. It was a favourite saying of his that there is always a way. The first time I heard him use the expression was after the failure of a patent depilatory which he promoted."

"Jeeves," I said, "what on earth are you talking about?"

"I mentioned Mr. Thistleton, sir, because his was in some respects a parallel case to the present one. His depilatory failed, but he did not despair. He put it on the market again under the name of Hair-o, guaranteed to produce a full crop of hair in a few months. It was advertised, if you remember, sir, by a humorous picture of a billiard-ball, before and after taking, and made such a substantial fortune that Mr. Thistleton was soon afterwards elevated to the peerage for services to his Party. It seems to me that, if Mr. Corcoran looks into the matter, he will find, like Mr. Thistleton, that there is always a way. Mr. Worple himself suggested the solution of the difficulty. In the heat of the moment he compared the portrait to an extract from a coloured comic supplement. I consider the suggestion a very valuable one, sir. Mr. Corcoran's portrait may not have pleased Mr. Worple as a likeness of his only child, but I have no doubt that editors would gladly consider it as a foundation for a series of humorous drawings. If Mr. Corcoran will allow me to make the suggestion, his talent has always been for the humorous. There is something about this picture—something bold and vigorous, which arrests the attention. I feel sure it would be highly popular."

Corky was glaring at the picture, and making a sort of dry, sucking noise with his mouth. He seemed completely overwrought.

And then suddenly he began to laugh in a wild way.

"Corky, old man!" I said, massaging him tenderly. I feared the poor blighter was hysterical.

He began to stagger about all over the floor.

"He's right! The man's absolutely right! Jeeves, you're a life-saver! You've hit on the greatest idea of the age! Report at the office on Monday! Start at the bottom of the business! I'll buy the business if I feel like it. I know the man who runs the comic section of the *Sunday Star*. He'll eat this thing. He was telling me only the other day how hard it was to get a good new series. He'll give me anything I ask for a real winner like this. I've got a gold-mine. Where's my hat? I've got an income for life! Where's that confounded hat? Lend me a fiver, Bertie. I want to take a taxi down to Park Row!"

Jeeves smiled paternally. Or, rather, he had a kind of paternal muscular spasm about the mouth, which is the nearest he ever gets to smiling.

"If I might make the suggestion, Mr. Corcoran—for a title of the series which you have in mind—'The Adventures of Baby Blobbs.'"

Corky and I looked at the picture, then at each other in an awed way. Jeeves was right. There could be no other title.

"Jeeves," I said. It was a few weeks later, and I had just finished looking at the comic section of the *Sunday Star*. "I'm an optimist. I always have been. The older I get, the more I agree with Shakespeare and those poet Johnnies about it always being darkest before the dawn and there's a silver lining and what you lose on the swings you make up on the roundabouts. Look at Mr. Corcoran, for instance. There was a fellow, one would have said, clear up to the eyebrows in the soup. To all appearances he had got it right in the neck. Yet look at him now. Have you seen these pictures?"

"I took the liberty of glancing at them before bringing them to you, sir. Extremely diverting."

"They have made a big hit, you know."

"I anticipated it, sir."

I leaned back against the pillows.

"You know, Jeeves, you're a genius. You ought to be drawing a commission on these things."

"I have nothing to complain of in that respect, sir. Mr. Corcoran has been most generous. I am putting out the brown suit, sir."

"No, I think I'll wear the blue with the faint red stripe."

"Not the blue with the faint red stripe, sir."

"But I rather fancy myself in it."

"Not the blue with the faint red stripe, sir."

"Oh, all right, have it your own way."

"Very good, sir. Thank you, sir."

Of course, I know it's as bad as being henpecked; but then Jeeves is always right. You've got to consider that, you know. What?

CHAPTER - 2

JEEVES AND THE UNBIDDEN GUEST

I'm not absolutely certain of my facts, but I rather fancy it's Shakespeare—or, if not, it's some equally brainy lad—who says that it's always just when a chappie is feeling particularly top-hole, and more than usually braced with things in general that Fate sneaks up behind him with a bit of lead piping. There's no doubt the man's right. It's absolutely that way with me. Take, for instance, the fairly rummy matter of Lady Malvern and her son Wilmot. A moment before they turned up, I was just thinking how thoroughly all right everything was.

It was one of those topping mornings, and I had just climbed out from under the cold shower, feeling like a two-year-old. As a matter of fact, I was especially bucked just then because the day before I had asserted myself with Jeeves—absolutely asserted myself, don't you know. You see, the way things had been going on I was rapidly becoming a dashed serf. The man had jolly well oppressed me. I didn't so much mind when he made me give up one of my new suits, because, Jeeves's judgment about suits is sound. But I as near as a toucher rebelled when he wouldn't let me wear a pair of cloth-topped boots which I loved like a couple of brothers. And when he tried to tread on me like a worm in the matter of a hat, I jolly well put my foot down and showed him who was who. It's a long story, and I haven't time to tell you now, but the point is that he wanted me to wear the Longacre—as worn by John Drew—when I had set my heart on the Country Gentleman—as worn by another famous actor chappie—and the end of the matter was that, after a rather painful scene, I bought the Country Gentleman. So that's how things stood on this particular morning, and I was feeling kind of manly and independent.

Well, I was in the bathroom, wondering what there was going to be for breakfast while I massaged the good old spine with a rough towel and sang slightly, when there was a tap at the door. I stopped singing and opened the door an inch.

"What ho without there!"

"Lady Malvern wishes to see you, sir," said Jeeves.

"Eh?"

"Lady Malvern, sir. She is waiting in the sitting-room."

"Pull yourself together, Jeeves, my man," I said, rather severely, for I bar practical jokes before breakfast. "You know perfectly well there's no one waiting for me in the sitting-room. How could there be when it's barely ten o'clock yet?"

"I gathered from her ladyship, sir, that she had landed from an ocean liner at an early hour this morning."

This made the thing a bit more plausible. I remembered that when I had arrived in America about a year before, the proceedings had begun at some ghastly hour like six, and that I had been shot out on to a foreign shore considerably before eight.

"Who the deuce is Lady Malvern, Jeeves?"

"Her ladyship did not confide in me, sir."

"Is she alone?"

"Her ladyship is accompanied by a Lord Pershore, sir. I fancy that his lordship would be her ladyship's son."

"Oh, well, put out rich raiment of sorts, and I'll be dressing."

"Our heather-mixture lounge is in readiness, sir."

"Then lead me to it."

While I was dressing I kept trying to think who on earth Lady Malvern could be. It wasn't till I had climbed through the top of my shirt and was reaching out for the studs that I remembered.

"I've placed her, Jeeves. She's a pal of my Aunt Agatha."

"Indeed, sir?"

"Yes. I met her at lunch one Sunday before I left London. A very vicious specimen. Writes books. She wrote a book on social conditions in India when she came back from the Durbar."

"Yes, sir? Pardon me, sir, but not that tie!"

"Eh?"

"Not that tie with the heather-mixture lounge, sir!"

It was a shock to me. I thought I had quelled the fellow. It was rather a solemn moment. What I mean is, if I weakened now, all my good work the night before would be thrown away. I braced myself.

"What's wrong with this tie? I've seen you give it a nasty look before. Speak out like a man! What's the matter with it?"

"Too ornate, sir."

"Nonsense! A cheerful pink. Nothing more."

"Unsuitable, sir."

"Jeeves, this is the tie I wear!"

"Very good, sir."

Dashed unpleasant. I could see that the man was wounded. But I was firm. I tied the tie, got into the coat and waistcoat, and went into the sitting-room.

"Halloa! Halloa! Halloa!" I said. "What?"

"Ah! How do you do, Mr. Wooster? You have never met my son, Wilmot, I think? Motty, darling, this is Mr. Wooster."

Lady Malvern was a hearty, happy, healthy, overpowering sort of dashed female, not so very tall but making up for it by measuring about six feet from the O.P. to the Prompt Side. She fitted into my biggest arm-chair as if it had been built round her by someone who knew they were wearing arm-chairs tight about the hips that season. She had bright, bulging eyes and a lot of yellow hair, and when she spoke she showed about fifty-seven front teeth. She was one of those women who kind of numb a fellow's faculties. She made me feel as if I were ten years old and had been brought into the drawing-room in my Sunday clothes to say how-d'you-do. Altogether by no means the sort of thing a chappie would wish to find in his sitting-room before breakfast.

Motty, the son, was about twenty-three, tall and thin and meek-looking. He had the same yellow hair as his mother, but he wore it plastered down and parted in the middle. His eyes bulged, too, but they weren't bright. They were a dull grey with pink rims. His chin gave up the struggle about half-way down, and he didn't appear to have any eyelashes. A mild, furtive, sheepish sort of blighter, in short.

"Awfully glad to see you," I said. "So you've popped over, eh? Making a long stay in America?"

"About a month. Your aunt gave me your address and told me to be sure and call on you."

I was glad to hear this, as it showed that Aunt Agatha was beginning to come round a bit. There had been some unpleasantness a year before, when she had sent me over to New York to disentangle my Cousin Gussie from the clutches of a girl on the music-hall stage. When I tell you that by the time I had finished my operations, Gussie had not only married the girl but had gone on the stage himself, and was doing well, you'll understand that Aunt Agatha was upset to no small extent. I simply hadn't dared go back and face her, and it was a relief to find that time had healed the wound and all that sort of thing enough to make her tell her pals to look me up. What I mean is, much as I liked America, I didn't want to have England barred to me for the rest of my natural; and, believe me, England is a jolly sight too small for anyone to live in with Aunt Agatha, if she's really on the warpath. So I braced on hearing these kind words and smiled genially on the assemblage.

"Your aunt said that you would do anything that was in your power to be of assistance to us."

"Rather? Oh, rather! Absolutely!"

"Thank you so much. I want you to put dear Motty up for a little while."

I didn't get this for a moment.

"Put him up? For my clubs?"

"No, no! Darling Motty is essentially a home bird. Aren't you, Motty darling?"

Motty, who was sucking the knob of his stick, uncorked himself.

"Yes, mother," he said, and corked himself up again.

"I should not like him to belong to clubs. I mean put him up here. Have him to live with you while I am away."

These frightful words trickled out of her like honey. The woman simply didn't seem to understand the ghastly nature of her proposal. I gave Motty the swift east-to-west. He was sitting with his mouth nuzzling the stick, blinking at the wall. The thought of having this planted on me for an indefinite period appalled me. Absolutely appalled me, don't you know. I was just starting to say that the shot wasn't on the board at any price, and that the first sign Motty gave of trying to nestle into my little home I would yell for the police, when she went on, rolling placidly over me, as it were.

There was something about this woman that sapped a chappie's will-power.

"I am leaving New York by the midday train, as I have to pay a visit to Sing-Sing prison. I am extremely interested in prison conditions in America. After that I work my way gradually across to the coast, visiting the points of interest on the journey. You see, Mr. Wooster, I am in America principally on business. No doubt you read my book, *India and the Indians*? My publishers are anxious for me to write a companion volume on the United States. I shall not be able to spend more than a month in the country, as I have to get back for the season, but a month should be ample. I was less than a month in India, and my dear friend Sir Roger Cremorne wrote his *America from Within* after a stay of only two weeks. I should love to take dear Motty with me, but the poor boy gets so sick when he travels by train. I shall have to pick him up on my return."

From where I sat I could see Jeeves in the dining-room, laying the breakfast-table. I wished I could have had a minute with him alone. I felt certain that he would have been able to think of some way of putting a stop to this woman.

"It will be such a relief to know that Motty is safe with you, Mr. Wooster. I know what the temptations of a great city are. Hitherto dear Motty has been sheltered from them. He has lived quietly with me in the country. I know that you will look after him carefully, Mr. Wooster. He will give very little trouble." She talked about the poor blighter as if he wasn't there. Not that Motty seemed to mind. He had stopped chewing his walking-stick and was sitting there with his mouth open. "He is a vegetarian and a teetotaller and is devoted to reading. Give him a nice book and he will be quite contented." She got up. "Thank you so much, Mr. Wooster! I don't know what I should have done without your help. Come, Motty! We have just time to see a few of the sights before my train goes. But I shall have to rely on you for most of my information about New York, darling. Be sure to keep your eyes open and take notes of your impressions! It will be such a help. Good-bye, Mr. Wooster. I will send Motty back early in the afternoon."

They went out, and I howled for Jeeves.

"Jeeves! What about it?"

"Sir?"

"What's to be done? You heard it all, didn't you? You were in the dining-room most of the time. That pill is coming to stay here."

"Pill, sir?"

"The excrescence."

"I beg your pardon, sir?"

I looked at Jeeves sharply. This sort of thing wasn't like him. It was as if he were deliberately trying to give me the pip. Then I understood. The man was really upset about that tie. He was trying to get his own back.

"Lord Pershore will be staying here from to-night, Jeeves," I said coldly.

"Very good, sir. Breakfast is ready, sir."

I could have sobbed into the bacon and eggs. That there wasn't any sympathy to be got out of Jeeves was what put the lid on it. For a moment I almost weakened and told him to destroy the hat and tie if he didn't like them, but I pulled myself together again. I was dashed if I was going to let Jeeves treat me like a bally one-man chain-gang!

But, what with brooding on Jeeves and brooding on Motty, I was in a pretty reduced sort of state. The more I examined the situation, the more blighted it became. There was nothing I could do. If I slung Motty out, he would report to his mother, and she would pass it on to Aunt Agatha, and I didn't like to think what would happen then. Sooner or later, I should be wanting to go back to England, and I didn't want to get there and find Aunt Agatha waiting on the quay for me with a stuffed eelskin. There was absolutely nothing for it but to put the fellow up and make the best of it.

About midday Motty's luggage arrived, and soon afterward a large parcel of what I took to be nice books. I brightened up a little when I saw it. It was one of those massive parcels and looked as if it had enough in it to keep the chappie busy for a year. I felt a trifle more cheerful, and I got my Country Gentleman hat and stuck it on my head, and gave the pink tie a twist, and reeled out to take a bite of lunch with one or two of the lads at a neighbouring hostelry; and what with excellent browsing and sluicing and cheery conversation and what-not, the afternoon passed quite happily. By dinner-time I had almost forgotten blighted Motty's existence.

I dined at the club and looked in at a show afterward, and it wasn't till fairly late that I got back to the flat. There were no signs of Motty, and I took it that he had gone to bed.

It seemed rummy to me, though, that the parcel of nice books was still there with the string and paper on it. It looked as if Motty, after seeing mother off at the station, had decided to call it a day.

Jeeves came in with the nightly whisky-and-soda. I could tell by the chappie's manner that he was still upset.

"Lord Pershore gone to bed, Jeeves?" I asked, with reserved hauteur and what-not.

"No, sir. His lordship has not yet returned."

"Not returned? What do you mean?"

"His lordship came in shortly after six-thirty, and, having dressed, went out again."

At this moment there was a noise outside the front door, a sort of scrabbling noise, as if somebody were trying to paw his way through the woodwork. Then a sort of thud.

"Better go and see what that is, Jeeves."

"Very good, sir."

He went out and came back again.

"If you would not mind stepping this way, sir, I think we might be able to carry him in."

"Carry him in?"

"His lordship is lying on the mat, sir."

I went to the front door. The man was right. There was Motty huddled up outside on the floor. He was moaning a bit.

"He's had some sort of dashed fit," I said. I took another look. "Jeeves! Someone's been feeding him meat!"

"Sir?"

"He's a vegetarian, you know. He must have been digging into a steak or something. Call up a doctor!"

"I hardly think it will be necessary, sir. If you would take his lordship's legs, while I——"

"Great Scot, Jeeves! You don't think—he can't be——"

"I am inclined to think so, sir."

And, by Jove, he was right! Once on the right track, you couldn't mistake it. Motty was under the surface.

It was the deuce of a shock.

"You never can tell, Jeeves!"

"Very seldom, sir."

"Remove the eye of authority and where are you?"

"Precisely, sir."

"Where is my wandering boy to-night and all that sort of thing, what?"

"It would seem so, sir."

"Well, we had better bring him in, eh?"

"Yes, sir."

So we lugged him in, and Jeeves put him to bed, and I lit a cigarette and sat down to think the thing over. I had a kind of foreboding. It seemed to me that I had let myself in for something pretty rocky.

Next morning, after I had sucked down a thoughtful cup of tea, I went into Motty's room to investigate. I expected to find the fellow a wreck, but there he was, sitting up in bed, quite chirpy, reading Gingery stories.

"What ho!" I said.

"What ho!" said Motty.

"What ho! What ho!"

"What ho! What ho! What ho!"

After that it seemed rather difficult to go on with the conversation.

"How are you feeling this morning?" I asked.

"Topping!" replied Motty, blithely and with abandon. "I say, you know, that fellow of yours—Jeeves, you know—is a corker. I had a most frightful headache when I woke up, and he brought me a sort of rummy dark drink, and it put me right again at once. Said it was his own invention. I must see more of that lad. He seems to me distinctly one of the ones!"

I couldn't believe that this was the same blighter who had sat and sucked his stick the day before.

"You ate something that disagreed with you last night, didn't you?" I said, by way of giving him a chance to slide out of it if he wanted to. But he wouldn't have it, at any price.

"No!" he replied firmly. "I didn't do anything of the kind. I drank too much! Much too much. Lots and lots too much! And, what's more, I'm going to do it again! I'm going to do it every night. If ever you see me sober, old top," he said, with a kind of holy exaltation, "tap me on the shoulder and say, 'Tut! Tut!' and I'll apologize and remedy the defect."

"But I say, you know, what about me?"

"What about you?"

"Well, I'm so to speak, as it were, kind of responsible for you. What I mean to say is, if you go doing this sort of thing I'm apt to get in the soup somewhat."

"I can't help your troubles," said Motty firmly. "Listen to me, old thing: this is the first time in my life that I've had a real chance to yield to the temptations of a great city. What's the use of a great city having temptations if fellows don't yield to them? Makes it so bally discouraging for a great city. Besides, mother told me to keep my eyes open and collect impressions."

I sat on the edge of the bed. I felt dizzy.

"I know just how you feel, old dear," said Motty consolingly. "And, if my principles would permit it, I would simmer down for your sake. But duty first! This is the first time I've been let out alone, and I mean to make the most of it. We're only young once. Why interfere with life's morning? Young man, rejoice in thy youth! Tra-la! What ho!"

Put like that, it did seem reasonable.

"All my bally life, dear boy," Motty went on, "I've been cooped up in the ancestral home at Much Middlefold, in Shropshire, and till you've been cooped up in Much Middlefold you don't know what cooping is! The only time we get any excitement is when one of the choir-boys is caught sucking chocolate during the sermon. When that happens, we talk about it for days. I've got about a month of New York, and I mean to store up a few happy memories for the long winter evenings. This is my only chance to collect a past, and I'm going to do it. Now tell me, old sport, as man to man, how does one get in touch with that very decent chappie Jeeves? Does one ring a bell or shout a bit? I should like to discuss the subject of a good stiff b.-and-s. with him!"

I had had a sort of vague idea, don't you know, that if I stuck close to Motty and went about the place with him, I might act as a bit of a damper on the gaiety. What I mean is, I thought that if, when he was being the life and soul of the party, he were to catch my reproving eye he might ease up a trifle on the revelry. So the next night I took him along to supper with me. It was the last time. I'm a quiet, peaceful sort of chappie who has lived all his life in London, and I can't stand the pace these swift sportsmen from the rural districts set. What I mean to say is this, I'm all for rational enjoyment and so forth, but I think a chappie makes himself conspicuous when he throws soft-boiled eggs at the electric fan. And decent mirth and all that sort of thing are all right, but I do bar dancing on tables and having to dash all over the place dodging waiters, managers, and chuckers-out, just when you want to sit still and digest.

Directly I managed to tear myself away that night and get home, I made up my mind that this was jolly well the last time that I went about with Motty. The only time I met him late at night after that was once when I passed the door of a fairly low-down sort of restaurant and had to step aside to dodge him as he sailed through the air *en route* for the opposite pavement, with a muscular sort of looking chappie peering out after him with a kind of gloomy satisfaction.

In a way, I couldn't help sympathizing with the fellow. He had about four weeks to have the good time that ought to have been spread over about ten years, and I didn't wonder at his wanting to be pretty busy. I should have been just the same in his place. Still, there was no denying that it was a bit thick. If it hadn't been for the thought of Lady Malvern and Aunt Agatha in the background, I should have regarded Motty's rapid work with an indulgent smile. But I couldn't get rid of the feeling that, sooner or later, I was the lad who was scheduled to get it behind the ear. And what with brooding on this prospect, and sitting up in the old flat waiting for the familiar footstep, and putting it to bed when it got there, and stealing into the sick-chamber next morning to contemplate the wreckage, I was beginning to lose weight. Absolutely becoming the good old shadow, I give you my honest word. Starting at sudden noises and what-not.

And no sympathy from Jeeves. That was what cut me to the quick. The man was still thoroughly pipped about the hat and tie, and simply wouldn't rally round. One morning I wanted comforting so much that I sank the pride of the Woosters and appealed to the fellow direct.

"Jeeves," I said, "this is getting a bit thick!"

"Sir?" Business and cold respectfulness.

"You know what I mean. This lad seems to have chucked all the principles of a well-spent boyhood. He has got it up his nose!"

"Yes, sir."

"Well, I shall get blamed, don't you know. You know what my Aunt Agatha is!"

"Yes, sir."

"Very well, then."

I waited a moment, but he wouldn't unbend.

"Jeeves," I said, "haven't you any scheme up your sleeve for coping with this blighter?"

"No, sir."

And he shimmered off to his lair. Obstinate devil! So dashed absurd, don't you know. It wasn't as if there was anything wrong with that Country Gentleman hat. It was a remarkably priceless effort, and much admired by the lads. But, just because he preferred the Longacre, he left me flat.

It was shortly after this that young Motty got the idea of bringing pals back in the small hours to continue the gay revels in the home. This was where I began to crack under the strain. You see, the part of town where I was living wasn't the right place for that sort of thing. I knew lots of chappies down Washington Square way who started the evening at about 2 a.m.—artists and writers and what-not, who frolicked considerably till checked by the arrival of the morning milk. That was all right. They like that sort of thing down there. The neighbours can't get to sleep unless there's someone dancing Hawaiian dances over their heads. But on Fifty-seventh Street the atmosphere wasn't right, and when Motty turned up at three in the morning with a collection of hearty lads, who only stopped singing their college song when they started singing "The Old Oaken Bucket," there was a marked peevishness among the old settlers in the flats. The management was extremely terse over the telephone at breakfast-time, and took a lot of soothing.

The next night I came home early, after a lonely dinner at a place which I'd chosen because there didn't seem any chance of meeting Motty there. The sitting-room was quite dark, and I was just moving to switch on the light, when there was a sort of explosion and something collared hold of my trouser-leg. Living with Motty had reduced me to such an extent that I was simply unable to cope with this thing. I jumped backward with a loud yell of anguish, and tumbled out into the hall just as Jeeves came out of his den to see what the matter was.

"Did you call, sir?"

"Jeeves! There's something in there that grabs you by the leg!"

"That would be Rollo, sir."

"Eh?"

"I would have warned you of his presence, but I did not hear you come in. His temper is a little uncertain at present, as he has not yet settled down."

"Who the deuce is Rollo?"

"His lordship's bull-terrier, sir. His lordship won him in a raffle, and tied him to the leg of the table. If you will allow me, sir, I will go in and switch on the light."

There really is nobody like Jeeves. He walked straight into the sitting-room, the biggest feat since Daniel and the lions' den, without a quiver. What's more, his magnetism or whatever they call it was such that the dashed animal, instead of pinning him by the leg, calmed down as if he had had a bromide, and rolled over on his back with all his paws in the air. If Jeeves had been his rich uncle he couldn't have been more chummy. Yet directly he caught sight of me again, he got all worked up and seemed to have only one idea in life—to start chewing me where he had left off.

"Rollo is not used to you yet, sir," said Jeeves, regarding the bally quadruped in an admiring sort of way. "He is an excellent watchdog."

"I don't want a watchdog to keep me out of my rooms."

"No, sir."

"Well, what am I to do?"

"No doubt in time the animal will learn to discriminate, sir. He will learn to distinguish your peculiar scent."

"What do you mean—my peculiar scent? Correct the impression that I intend to hang about in the hall while life slips by, in the hope that one of these days that dashed animal will decide that I smell all right." I thought for a bit. "Jeeves!"

"Sir?"

"I'm going away—to-morrow morning by the first train. I shall go and stop with Mr. Todd in the country."

"Do you wish me to accompany you, sir?"

"No."

"Very good, sir."

"I don't know when I shall be back. Forward my letters."

"Yes, sir."

As a matter of fact, I was back within the week. Rocky Todd, the pal I went to stay with, is a rummy sort of a chap who lives all alone in the wilds of Long Island, and likes it; but a little of that sort of thing goes a long way with me. Dear old Rocky is one of the best, but after a few days in his cottage in the woods, miles away from anywhere, New York, even with Motty on the premises, began to look pretty good to me. The days down on Long Island have forty-eight hours in them; you can't get to sleep at night because of the bellowing of the crickets; and you have to walk two miles for a drink and six for an evening paper. I thanked Rocky for his kind hospitality, and caught the only train they have down in those parts. It landed me in New York about dinner-time. I went straight to the old flat. Jeeves came out of his lair. I looked round cautiously for Rollo.

"Where's that dog, Jeeves? Have you got him tied up?"

"The animal is no longer here, sir. His lordship gave him to the porter, who sold him. His lordship took a prejudice against the animal on account of being bitten by him in the calf of the leg."

I don't think I've ever been so bucked by a bit of news. I felt I had misjudged Rollo. Evidently, when you got to know him better, he had a lot of intelligence in him.

"Ripping!" I said. "Is Lord Pershore in, Jeeves?"

"No, sir."

"Do you expect him back to dinner?"

"No, sir."

"Where is he?"

"In prison, sir."

Have you ever trodden on a rake and had the handle jump up and hit you? That's how I felt then.

"In prison!"

"Yes, sir."

"You don't mean—in prison?"

"Yes, sir."

I lowered myself into a chair.

"Why?" I said.

"He assaulted a constable, sir."

"Lord Pershore assaulted a constable!"

"Yes, sir."

I digested this.

"But, Jeeves, I say! This is frightful!"

"Sir?"

"What will Lady Malvern say when she finds out?"

"I do not fancy that her ladyship will find out, sir."

"But she'll come back and want to know where he is."

"I rather fancy, sir, that his lordship's bit of time will have run out by then."

"But supposing it hasn't?"

"In that event, sir, it may be judicious to prevaricate a little."

"How?"

"If I might make the suggestion, sir, I should inform her ladyship that his lordship has left for a short visit to Boston."

"Why Boston?"

"Very interesting and respectable centre, sir."

"Jeeves, I believe you've hit it."

"I fancy so, sir."

"Why, this is really the best thing that could have happened. If this hadn't turned up to prevent him, young Motty would have been in a sanatorium by the time Lady Malvern got back."

"Exactly, sir."

The more I looked at it in that way, the sounder this prison wheeze seemed to me. There was no doubt in the world that prison was just what the doctor ordered for Motty. It was the only thing that could have pulled him up. I was sorry for the poor blighter, but, after all, I reflected, a chappie who had lived all his life with Lady Malvern, in a small village in the interior of Shropshire, wouldn't have much to kick at in a prison. Altogether, I began to feel absolutely braced again. Life became like what the poet Johnnie says—one grand, sweet song. Things went on so comfortably and peacefully for a couple of weeks that I give you my word that I'd almost forgotten such a person as Motty existed. The only flaw in the scheme of things was that Jeeves was still pained and distant. It wasn't anything he said or did, mind you, but there was a rummy something about him all the time. Once when I was tying the pink tie I caught sight of him in the looking-glass. There was a kind of grieved look in his eye.

And then Lady Malvern came back, a good bit ahead of schedule. I hadn't been expecting her for days. I'd forgotten how time had been slipping along. She turned up one morning while I was still in bed sipping tea and thinking of this and that. Jeeves flowed in with the announcement that he had just loosed her into the sitting-room. I draped a few garments round me and went in.

There she was, sitting in the same arm-chair, looking as massive as ever. The only difference was that she didn't uncover the teeth, as she had done the first time.

"Good morning," I said. "So you've got back, what?"

"I have got back."

There was something sort of bleak about her tone, rather as if she had swallowed an east wind. This I took to be due to the fact that she probably hadn't breakfasted. It's only after a bit of breakfast that I'm able to regard the world with that sunny cheeriness which makes a fellow the universal favourite. I'm never much of a lad till I've engulfed an egg or two and a beaker of coffee.

"I suppose you haven't breakfasted?"

"I have not yet breakfasted."

"Won't you have an egg or something? Or a sausage or something? Or something?"

"No, thank you."

She spoke as if she belonged to an anti-sausage society or a league for the suppression of eggs. There was a bit of a silence.

"I called on you last night," she said, "but you were out."

"Awfully sorry! Had a pleasant trip?"

"Extremely, thank you."

"See everything? Niag'ra Falls, Yellowstone Park, and the jolly old Grand Canyon, and what-not?"

"I saw a great deal."

There was another slightly *frappé* silence. Jeeves floated silently into the dining-room and began to lay the breakfast-table.

"I hope Wilmot was not in your way, Mr. Wooster?"

I had been wondering when she was going to mention Motty.

"Rather not! Great pals! Hit it off splendidly."

"You were his constant companion, then?"

"Absolutely! We were always together. Saw all the sights, don't you know. We'd take in the Museum of Art in the morning, and have a bit of lunch at some good vegetarian place, and then toddle along to a sacred concert in the afternoon, and home to an early dinner. We usually played dominoes after dinner. And then the early bed and the refreshing sleep. We had a great time. I was awfully sorry when he went away to Boston."

"Oh! Wilmot is in Boston?"

"Yes. I ought to have let you know, but of course we didn't know where you were. You were dodging all over the place like a snipe—I mean, don't you know, dodging all over the place, and we couldn't get at you. Yes, Motty went off to Boston."

"You're sure he went to Boston?"

"Oh, absolutely." I called out to Jeeves, who was now messing about in the next room with forks and so forth: "Jeeves, Lord Pershore didn't change his mind about going to Boston, did he?"

"No, sir."

"I thought I was right. Yes, Motty went to Boston."

"Then how do you account, Mr. Wooster, for the fact that when I went yesterday afternoon to Blackwell's Island prison, to secure material for my book, I saw poor, dear Wilmot there, dressed in a striped suit, seated beside a pile of stones with a hammer in his hands?"

I tried to think of something to say, but nothing came. A chappie has to be a lot broader about the forehead than I am to handle a jolt like this. I strained the old bean till it creaked, but between the collar and the hair parting nothing stirred. I was dumb. Which was lucky, because I wouldn't have had a chance to get any persiflage out of my system. Lady Malvern collared the conversation. She had been bottling it up, and now it came out with a rush:

"So this is how you have looked after my poor, dear boy, Mr. Wooster! So this is how you have abused my trust! I left him in your charge, thinking that I could rely on you to shield him from evil. He came to you innocent, unversed in the ways of the world, confiding, unused to the temptations of a large city, and you led him astray!"

I hadn't any remarks to make. All I could think of was the picture of Aunt Agatha drinking all this in and reaching out to sharpen the hatchet against my return.

"You deliberately——"

Far away in the misty distance a soft voice spoke:

"If I might explain, your ladyship."

Jeeves had projected himself in from the dining-room and materialized on the rug. Lady Malvern tried to freeze him with a look, but you can't do that sort of thing to Jeeves. He is look-proof.

"I fancy, your ladyship, that you have misunderstood Mr. Wooster, and that he may have given you the impression that he was in New York when his lordship—was removed. When Mr. Wooster informed your ladyship that his lordship had gone to Boston, he was relying on the version I had given him of his lordship's movements. Mr. Wooster was away, visiting a friend in the country, at the time, and knew nothing of the matter till your ladyship informed him."

Lady Malvern gave a kind of grunt. It didn't rattle Jeeves.

"I feared Mr. Wooster might be disturbed if he knew the truth, as he is so attached to his lordship and has taken such pains to look after him, so I took the liberty of telling him that his lordship had gone away for a visit. It might have been hard for Mr. Wooster to believe that his lordship had gone to prison voluntarily and from the best motives, but your ladyship, knowing him better, will readily understand."

"What!" Lady Malvern goggled at him. "Did you say that Lord Pershore went to prison voluntarily?"

"If I might explain, your ladyship. I think that your ladyship's parting words made a deep impression on his lordship. I have frequently heard him speak to Mr. Wooster of his desire to do something to follow your ladyship's instructions and collect material for your ladyship's book on America. Mr. Wooster will bear me out when I say that his lordship was frequently extremely depressed at the thought that he was doing so little to help."

"Absolutely, by Jove! Quite pipped about it!" I said.

"The idea of making a personal examination into the prison system of the country—from within—occurred to his lordship very suddenly one night. He embraced it eagerly. There was no restraining him."

Lady Malvern looked at Jeeves, then at me, then at Jeeves again. I could see her struggling with the thing.

"Surely, your ladyship," said Jeeves, "it is more reasonable to suppose that a gentleman of his lordship's character went to prison of his own volition than that he committed some breach of the law which necessitated his arrest?"

Lady Malvern blinked. Then she got up.

"Mr. Wooster," she said, "I apologize. I have done you an injustice. I should have known Wilmot better. I should have had more faith in his pure, fine spirit."

"Absolutely!" I said.

"Your breakfast is ready, sir," said Jeeves.

I sat down and dallied in a dazed sort of way with a poached egg.

"Jeeves," I said, "you are certainly a life-saver!"

"Thank you, sir."

"Nothing would have convinced my Aunt Agatha that I hadn't lured that blighter into riotous living."

"I fancy you are right, sir."

I champed my egg for a bit. I was most awfully moved, don't you know, by the way Jeeves had rallied round. Something seemed to tell me that this was an occasion that called for rich rewards. For a moment I hesitated. Then I made up my mind.

"Jeeves!"

"Sir?"

"That pink tie!"

"Yes, sir?"

"Burn it!"

"Thank you, sir."

"And, Jeeves!"

"Yes, sir?"

"Take a taxi and get me that Longacre hat, as worn by John Drew!"

"Thank you very much, sir."

I felt most awfully braced. I felt as if the clouds had rolled away and all was as it used to be. I felt like one of those chappies in the novels who calls off the fight with his wife in the last chapter and decides to forget and forgive. I felt I wanted to do all sorts of other things to show Jeeves that I appreciated him.

"Jeeves," I said, "it isn't enough. Is there anything else you would like?"

"Yes, sir. If I may make the suggestion—fifty dollars."

"Fifty dollars?"

"It will enable me to pay a debt of honour, sir. I owe it to his lordship."

"You owe Lord Pershore fifty dollars?"

"Yes, sir. I happened to meet him in the street the night his lordship was arrested. I had been thinking a good deal about the most suitable method of inducing him to abandon his mode of living, sir. His lordship was a little over-excited at the time and I fancy that he mistook me for a friend of his. At any rate when I took the liberty of wagering him fifty dollars that he would not punch a passing policeman in the eye, he accepted the bet very cordially and won it."

I produced my pocket-book and counted out a hundred.

"Take this, Jeeves," I said; "fifty isn't enough. Do you know, Jeeves, you're—well, you absolutely stand alone!"

"I endeavour to give satisfaction, sir," said Jeeves.

CHAPTER - 3

JEEVES AND THE HARD-BOILED EGG

Sometimes of a morning, as I've sat in bed sucking down the early cup of tea and watched my man Jeeves flitting about the room and putting out the raiment for the day, I've wondered what the deuce I should do if the fellow ever took it into his head to leave me. It's not so bad now I'm in New York, but in London the anxiety was frightful. There used to be all sorts of attempts on the part of low blighters to sneak him away from me. Young Reggie Foljambe to my certain knowledge offered him double what I was giving him, and Alistair Bingham-Reeves, who's got a valet who had been known to press his trousers sideways, used to look at him, when he came to see me, with a kind of glittering hungry eye which disturbed me deucedly. Bally pirates!

The thing, you see, is that Jeeves is so dashed competent. You can spot it even in the way he shoves studs into a shirt.

I rely on him absolutely in every crisis, and he never lets me down. And, what's more, he can always be counted on to extend himself on behalf of any pal of mine who happens to be to all appearances knee-deep in the bouillon. Take the rather rummy case, for instance, of dear old Bicky and his uncle, the hard-boiled egg.

It happened after I had been in America for a few months. I got back to the flat latish one night, and when Jeeves brought me the final drink he said:

"Mr. Bickersteth called to see you this evening, sir, while you were out."

"Oh?" I said.

"Twice, sir. He appeared a trifle agitated."

"What, pipped?"

"He gave that impression, sir."

I sipped the whisky. I was sorry if Bicky was in trouble, but, as a matter of fact, I was rather glad to have something I could discuss freely with Jeeves just then, because things had been a bit strained between us for some time, and it had been rather difficult to hit on anything to talk about that wasn't apt to take a personal turn. You see, I had decided—rightly or wrongly—to grow a moustache and this had cut Jeeves to the quick. He couldn't stick the thing at any price, and I had been living ever since in an atmosphere of bally disapproval till I was getting jolly well fed up with it. What I mean is, while there's no doubt that in certain matters of dress Jeeves's judgment is absolutely sound and should be followed, it seemed to me that it was getting a bit too thick if he was going to edit my face as well as my costume. No one can call me an unreasonable chappie, and many's the time I've given in like a lamb when Jeeves has voted against one of my pet suits or ties; but when it comes to a valet's staking out a claim on your upper lip you've simply got to have a bit of the good old bulldog pluck and defy the blighter.

"He said that he would call again later, sir."

"Something must be up, Jeeves."

"Yes, sir."

I gave the moustache a thoughtful twirl. It seemed to hurt Jeeves a good deal, so I chucked it.

"I see by the paper, sir, that Mr. Bickersteth's uncle is arriving on the *Carmantic*."

"Yes?"

"His Grace the Duke of Chiswick, sir."

This was news to me, that Bicky's uncle was a duke. Rum, how little one knows about one's pals! I had met Bicky for the first time at a species of beano or jamboree down in Washington Square, not long after my arrival in New York. I suppose I was a bit homesick at the time, and I rather took to Bicky when I found that he was an Englishman and had, in fact, been up at Oxford with me. Besides, he was a frightful chump, so we naturally drifted together; and while we were taking a quiet snort in a corner that wasn't all cluttered up with artists and sculptors and what-not, he furthermore endeared himself to me by a most extraordinarily gifted imitation of a bull-terrier chasing a cat up a tree. But, though we had subsequently become extremely pally, all I really knew about him was that he was generally hard up, and had an uncle who relieved the strain a bit from time to time by sending him monthly remittances.

"If the Duke of Chiswick is his uncle," I said, "why hasn't he a title? Why isn't he Lord What-Not?"

"Mr. Bickersteth is the son of his grace's late sister, sir, who married Captain Rollo Bickersteth of the Coldstream Guards."

Jeeves knows everything.

"Is Mr. Bickersteth's father dead, too?"

"Yes, sir."

"Leave any money?"

"No, sir."

I began to understand why poor old Bicky was always more or less on the rocks. To the casual and irreflective observer, if you know what I mean, it may sound a pretty good wheeze having a duke for an uncle, but the trouble about old Chiswick was that, though an extremely wealthy old buster, owning half London and about five counties up north, he was notoriously the most prudent spender in England. He was what American chappies would call a hard-boiled egg. If Bicky's people hadn't left him anything and he depended on what he could prise out of the old duke, he was in a pretty bad way. Not that that explained why he was hunting me like this, because he was a chap who never borrowed money. He said he wanted to keep his pals, so never bit any one's ear on principle.

At this juncture the door bell rang. Jeeves floated out to answer it.

"Yes, sir. Mr. Wooster has just returned," I heard him say. And Bicky came trickling in, looking pretty sorry for himself.

"Halloa, Bicky!" I said. "Jeeves told me you had been trying to get me. Jeeves, bring another glass, and let the revels commence. What's the trouble, Bicky?"

"I'm in a hole, Bertie. I want your advice."

"Say on, old lad!"

"My uncle's turning up to-morrow, Bertie."

"So Jeeves told me."

"The Duke of Chiswick, you know."

"So Jeeves told me."

Bicky seemed a bit surprised.

"Jeeves seems to know everything."

"Rather rummily, that's exactly what I was thinking just now myself."

"Well, I wish," said Bicky gloomily, "that he knew a way to get me out of the hole I'm in."

Jeeves shimmered in with the glass, and stuck it competently on the table.

"Mr. Bickersteth is in a bit of a hole, Jeeves," I said, "and wants you to rally round."

"Very good, sir."

Bicky looked a bit doubtful.

"Well, of course, you know, Bertie, this thing is by way of being a bit private and all that."

"I shouldn't worry about that, old top. I bet Jeeves knows all about it already. Don't you, Jeeves?"

"Yes, sir."

"Eh!" said Bicky, rattled.

"I am open to correction, sir, but is not your dilemma due to the fact that you are at a loss to explain to his grace why you are in New York instead of in Colorado?"

Bicky rocked like a jelly in a high wind.

"How the deuce do you know anything about it?"

"I chanced to meet his grace's butler before we left England. He informed me that he happened to overhear his grace speaking to you on the matter, sir, as he passed the library door."

Bicky gave a hollow sort of laugh.

"Well, as everybody seems to know all about it, there's no need to try to keep it dark. The old boy turfed me out, Bertie, because he said I was a brainless nincompoop. The idea was that he would give me a remittance on condition that I dashed out to some blighted locality of the name of Colorado and learned farming or ranching, or whatever they call it, at some bally ranch or farm or whatever it's called. I didn't fancy the idea a bit. I should have had to ride horses and pursue cows, and so forth. I hate horses. They bite at you. I was all against the scheme. At the same time, don't you know, I had to have that remittance."

"I get you absolutely, dear boy."

"Well, when I got to New York it looked a decent sort of place to me, so I thought it would be a pretty sound notion to stop here. So I cabled to my uncle telling him that I had dropped into a good business wheeze in the city and wanted to chuck the ranch idea. He wrote back that it was all right, and here I've been ever since. He thinks I'm doing well at something or other over here. I never dreamed, don't you know, that he would ever come out here. What on earth am I to do?"

"Jeeves," I said, "what on earth is Mr. Bickersteth to do?"

"You see," said Bicky, "I had a wireless from him to say that he was coming to stay with me—to save hotel bills, I suppose. I've always given him the impression that I was living in pretty good style. I can't have him to stay at my boarding-house."

"Thought of anything, Jeeves?" I said.

"To what extent, sir, if the question is not a delicate one, are you prepared to assist Mr. Bickersteth?"

"I'll do anything I can for you, of course, Bicky, old man."

"Then, if I might make the suggestion, sir, you might lend Mr. Bickersteth—

"No, by Jove!" said Bicky firmly. "I never have touched you, Bertie, and I'm not going to start now. I may be a chump, but it's my boast that I don't owe a penny to a single soul—not counting tradesmen, of course."

"I was about to suggest, sir, that you might lend Mr. Bickersteth this flat. Mr. Bickersteth could give his grace the impression that he was the owner of it. With your permission I could convey the notion that I was in Mr. Bickersteth's employment, and not in yours. You would be residing here temporarily as Mr. Bickersteth's guest. His grace would occupy the second spare bedroom. I fancy that you would find this answer satisfactorily, sir."

Bicky had stopped rocking himself and was staring at Jeeves in an awed sort of way.

"I would advocate the dispatching of a wireless message to his grace on board the vessel, notifying him of the change of address. Mr. Bickersteth could meet his grace at the dock and proceed directly here. Will that meet the situation, sir?"

"Absolutely."

"Thank you, sir."

Bicky followed him with his eye till the door closed.

"How does he do it, Bertie?" he said. "I'll tell you what I think it is. I believe it's something to do with the shape of his head. Have you ever noticed his head, Bertie, old man? It sort of sticks out at the back!"

I hopped out of bed early next morning, so as to be among those present when the old boy should arrive. I knew from experience that these ocean liners fetch up at the dock at a deucedly ungodly hour. It wasn't much after nine by the time I'd dressed and had my morning tea and was leaning out of the window, watching the street for Bicky and his uncle. It was one of those jolly, peaceful mornings that make a chappie wish he'd got a soul or something, and I was just brooding on life in general when I became aware of the dickens of a spate in progress down below. A taxi had driven up, and an old boy in a top hat had got out and was kicking up a frightful row about the fare. As far as I could make out, he was trying to get the cab chappie to switch from New York to London prices, and the cab chappie had apparently never heard of London before, and didn't seem to think a lot of it now. The old boy said that in London the trip would have set him back eightpence; and the cabby said he should worry. I called to Jeeves.

"The duke has arrived, Jeeves."

"Yes, sir?"

"That'll be him at the door now."

Jeeves made a long arm and opened the front door, and the old boy crawled in, looking licked to a splinter.

"How do you do, sir?" I said, bustling up and being the ray of sunshine. "Your nephew went down to the dock to meet you, but you must have missed him. My name's Wooster, don't you know. Great pal of Bicky's, and all that sort of thing. I'm staying with him, you know. Would you like a cup of tea? Jeeves, bring a cup of tea."

Old Chiswick had sunk into an arm-chair and was looking about the room.

"Does this luxurious flat belong to my nephew Francis?"

"Absolutely."

"It must be terribly expensive."

"Pretty well, of course. Everything costs a lot over here, you know."

He moaned. Jeeves filtered in with the tea. Old Chiswick took a stab at it to restore his tissues, and nodded.

"A terrible country, Mr. Wooster! A terrible country! Nearly eight shillings for a short cab-drive! Iniquitous!" He took another look round the room. It seemed to fascinate him. "Have you any idea how much my nephew pays for this flat, Mr. Wooster?"

"About two hundred dollars a month, I believe."

"What! Forty pounds a month!"

I began to see that, unless I made the thing a bit more plausible, the scheme might turn out a frost. I could guess what the old boy was thinking. He was trying to square all this prosperity with what he knew of poor old Bicky. And one had to admit that it took a lot of squaring, for dear old Bicky, though a stout fellow and absolutely unrivalled as an imitator of bull-terriers and cats, was in many ways one of the most pronounced fatheads that ever pulled on a suit of gent's underwear.

"I suppose it seems rummy to you," I said, "but the fact is New York often bucks chappies up and makes them show a flash of speed that you wouldn't have imagined them capable of. It sort of develops them. Something in the air, don't you know. I imagine that Bicky in the past, when you knew him, may have been something of a chump, but it's quite different now. Devilish efficient sort of chappie, and looked on in commercial circles as quite the nib!"

"I am amazed! What is the nature of my nephew's business, Mr. Wooster?"

"Oh, just business, don't you know. The same sort of thing Carnegie and Rockefeller and all these coves do, you know." I slid for the door. "Awfully sorry to leave you, but I've got to meet some of the lads elsewhere."

Coming out of the lift I met Bicky bustling in from the street.

"Halloa, Bertie! I missed him. Has he turned up?"

"He's upstairs now, having some tea."

"What does he think of it all?"

"He's absolutely rattled."

"Ripping! I'll be toddling up, then. Toodle-oo, Bertie, old man. See you later."

"Pip-pip, Bicky, dear boy."

He trotted off, full of merriment and good cheer, and I went off to the club to sit in the window and watch the traffic coming up one way and going down the other.

It was latish in the evening when I looked in at the flat to dress for dinner.

"Where's everybody, Jeeves?" I said, finding no little feet pattering about the place. "Gone out?"

"His grace desired to see some of the sights of the city, sir. Mr. Bickersteth is acting as his escort. I fancy their immediate objective was Grant's Tomb."

"I suppose Mr. Bickersteth is a bit braced at the way things are going—what?"

"Sir?"

"I say, I take it that Mr. Bickersteth is tolerably full of beans."

"Not altogether, sir."

"What's his trouble now?"

"The scheme which I took the liberty of suggesting to Mr. Bickersteth and yourself has, unfortunately, not answered entirely satisfactorily, sir."

"Surely the duke believes that Mr. Bickersteth is doing well in business, and all that sort of thing?"

"Exactly, sir. With the result that he has decided to cancel Mr. Bickersteth's monthly allowance, on the ground that, as Mr. Bickersteth is doing so well on his own account, he no longer requires pecuniary assistance."

"Great Scot, Jeeves! This is awful."

"Somewhat disturbing, sir."

"I never expected anything like this!"

"I confess I scarcely anticipated the contingency myself, sir."

"I suppose it bowled the poor blighter over absolutely?"

"Mr. Bickersteth appeared somewhat taken aback, sir."

My heart bled for Bicky.

"We must do something, Jeeves."

"Yes, sir."

"Can you think of anything?"

"Not at the moment, sir."

"There must be something we can do."

"It was a maxim of one of my former employers, sir—as I believe I mentioned to you once before—the present Lord Bridgnorth, that there is always a way. I remember his lordship using the expression on the occasion—he was then a business gentleman and had not yet received his title—when a patent hair-restorer which he chanced to be promoting failed to attract the public. He put it on the market under another name as a depilatory, and amassed a substantial fortune. I have generally found his lordship's aphorism based on sound foundations. No doubt we shall be able to discover some solution of Mr. Bickersteth's difficulty, sir."

"Well, have a stab at it, Jeeves!"

"I will spare no pains, sir."

I went and dressed sadly. It will show you pretty well how pipped I was when I tell you that I near as a toucher put on a white tie with a dinner-jacket. I sallied out for a bit of food more to pass the time than because I wanted it. It seemed brutal to be wading into the bill of fare with poor old Bicky headed for the breadline.

When I got back old Chiswick had gone to bed, but Bicky was there, hunched up in an arm-chair, brooding pretty tensely, with a cigarette hanging out of the corner of his mouth and a more or less glassy stare in his eyes. He had the aspect of one who had been soaked with what the newspaper chappies call "some blunt instrument."

"This is a bit thick, old thing—what!" I said.

He picked up his glass and drained it feverishly, overlooking the fact that it hadn't anything in it.

"I'm done, Bertie!" he said.

He had another go at the glass. It didn't seem to do him any good.

"If only this had happened a week later, Bertie! My next month's money was due to roll in on Saturday. I could have worked a wheeze I've been reading about in the magazine advertisements. It seems that you can make a dashed amount of money if you can only collect a few dollars and start a chicken-farm. Jolly sound scheme, Bertie! Say you buy a hen—call it one hen for the sake of argument. It lays an egg every day of the week. You sell the eggs seven for twenty-five cents. Keep of hen costs nothing. Profit practically twenty-five cents on every seven eggs. Or look at it another way: Suppose you have a dozen eggs. Each of the hens has a dozen chickens. The chickens grow up and have more chickens. Why, in no time you'd have the place covered knee-deep in hens, all laying eggs, at twenty-five cents for every seven. You'd make a fortune. Jolly life, too, keeping hens!" He had begun to get quite worked up at the thought of it, but he slopped back in his chair at this juncture with a good deal of gloom. "But, of course, it's no good," he said, "because I haven't the cash."

"You've only to say the word, you know, Bicky, old top."

"Thanks awfully, Bertie, but I'm not going to sponge on you."

That's always the way in this world. The chappies you'd like to lend money to won't let you, whereas the chappies you don't want to lend it to will do everything except actually stand you on your head and lift the specie out of your pockets. As a lad who has always rolled tolerably free in the right stuff, I've had lots of experience of the second class. Many's the time, back in London, I've hurried along Piccadilly and felt the hot breath of the toucher on the back of my neck and heard his sharp, excited yapping as he closed in on me. I've simply spent my life scattering largesse to blighters I didn't care a hang for; yet here was I now, dripping doubloons and pieces of eight and longing to hand them over, and Bicky, poor fish, absolutely on his uppers, not taking any at any price.

"Well, there's only one hope, then."

"What's that?"

"Jeeves."

"Sir?"

There was Jeeves, standing behind me, full of zeal. In this matter of shimmering into rooms the chappie is rummy to a degree. You're sitting in the old arm-chair, thinking of this and that, and then suddenly you look up, and there he is. He moves from point to point with as little uproar as a jelly fish. The thing startled poor old Bicky considerably. He rose from his seat like a rocketing pheasant. I'm used to Jeeves now, but often in the days when he first came to me I've bitten my tongue freely on finding him unexpectedly in my midst.

"Did you call, sir?"

"Oh, there you are, Jeeves!"

"Precisely, sir."

"Jeeves, Mr. Bickersteth is still up the pole. Any ideas?"

"Why, yes, sir. Since we had our recent conversation I fancy I have found what may prove a solution. I do not wish to appear to be taking a liberty, sir, but I think that we have overlooked his grace's potentialities as a source of revenue."

Bicky laughed, what I have sometimes seen described as a hollow, mocking laugh, a sort of bitter cackle from the back of the throat, rather like a gargle.

"I do not allude, sir," explained Jeeves, "to the possibility of inducing his grace to part with money. I am taking the liberty of regarding his grace in the light of an at present—if I may say so—useless property, which is capable of being developed."

Bicky looked at me in a helpless kind of way. I'm bound to say I didn't get it myself.

"Couldn't you make it a bit easier, Jeeves!"

"In a nutshell, sir, what I mean is this: His grace is, in a sense, a prominent personage. The inhabitants of this country, as no doubt you are aware, sir, are peculiarly addicted to shaking hands with prominent personages. It occurred to me that Mr. Bickersteth or yourself might know of persons who would be willing to pay a small fee—let us say two dollars or three—for the privilege of an introduction, including handshake, to his grace."

Bicky didn't seem to think much of it.

"Do you mean to say that anyone would be mug enough to part with solid cash just to shake hands with my uncle?"

"I have an aunt, sir, who paid five shillings to a young fellow for bringing a moving-picture actor to tea at her house one Sunday. It gave her social standing among the neighbours."

Bicky wavered.

"If you think it could be done——"

"I feel convinced of it, sir."

"What do you think, Bertie?"

"I'm for it, old boy, absolutely. A very brainy wheeze."

"Thank you, sir. Will there be anything further? Good night, sir."

And he floated out, leaving us to discuss details.

Until we started this business of floating old Chiswick as a money-making proposition I had never realized what a perfectly foul time those Stock Exchange chappies must have when the public isn't biting freely. Nowadays I read that bit they put in the financial reports about "The market opened quietly" with a sympathetic eye, for, by Jove, it certainly opened quietly for us! You'd hardly believe how difficult it was to interest the public and make them take a flutter on the old boy. By the end of the week the only name we had on our list was a delicatessen-store keeper down in Bicky's part of the town, and as he wanted us to take it out in sliced ham instead of cash that didn't help much. There was a gleam of light when the brother of Bicky's pawnbroker offered ten dollars, money down, for an introduction to old Chiswick, but the deal fell through, owing to its turning out that the chap was an anarchist and intended to kick the old boy instead of shaking hands with him. At that, it took me the deuce of a time to persuade Bicky not to grab the cash and let things take their course. He seemed to regard the pawnbroker's brother rather as a sportsman and benefactor of his species than otherwise.

The whole thing, I'm inclined to think, would have been off if it hadn't been for Jeeves. There is no doubt that Jeeves is in a class of his own. In the matter of brain and resource I don't think I have ever met a chappie so supremely like mother made. He trickled into my room one morning with a good old cup of tea, and intimated that there was something doing.

"Might I speak to you with regard to that matter of his grace, sir?"

"It's all off. We've decided to chuck it."

"Sir?"

"It won't work. We can't get anybody to come."

"I fancy I can arrange that aspect of the matter, sir."

"Do you mean to say you've managed to get anybody?"

"Yes, sir. Eighty-seven gentlemen from Birdsburg, sir."

I sat up in bed and spilt the tea.

"Birdsburg?"

"Birdsburg, Missouri, sir."

"How did you get them?"

"I happened last night, sir, as you had intimated that you would be absent from home, to attend a theatrical performance, and entered into conversation between the acts with the occupant of the adjoining seat. I had observed that he was wearing a somewhat ornate decoration in his buttonhole, sir—a large blue button with the words 'Boost for Birdsburg' upon it in red letters, scarcely a judicious addition to a gentleman's evening costume. To my surprise I noticed that the auditorium was full of persons similarly decorated. I ventured to inquire the explanation, and was informed that these gentlemen, forming a party of eighty-seven, are a convention from a town of the name if Birdsburg, in the State of Missouri. Their visit, I gathered, was purely of a social and pleasurable nature, and my informant spoke at some length of the entertainments arranged for their stay in the city. It was when he related with a considerable amount of satisfaction and pride, that a deputation of their number had been introduced to and had shaken hands with a well-known prizefighter, that it occurred to me to broach the subject of his grace. To make a long story short, sir, I have arranged, subject to your approval, that the entire convention shall be presented to his grace to-morrow afternoon."

I was amazed. This chappie was a Napoleon.

"Eighty-seven, Jeeves. At how much a head?"

"I was obliged to agree to a reduction for quantity, sir. The terms finally arrived at were one hundred and fifty dollars for the party."

I thought a bit.

"Payable in advance?"

"No, sir. I endeavoured to obtain payment in advance, but was not successful."

"Well, any way, when we get it I'll make it up to five hundred. Bicky'll never know. Do you suspect Mr. Bickersteth would suspect anything, Jeeves, if I made it up to five hundred?"

"I fancy not, sir. Mr. Bickersteth is an agreeable gentleman, but not bright."

"All right, then. After breakfast run down to the bank and get me some money."

"Yes, sir."

"You know, you're a bit of a marvel, Jeeves."

"Thank you, sir."

"Right-o!"

"Very good, sir."

When I took dear old Bicky aside in the course of the morning and told him what had happened he nearly broke down. He tottered into the sitting-room and buttonholed old Chiswick, who was reading the comic section of the morning paper with a kind of grim resolution.

"Uncle," he said, "are you doing anything special to-morrow afternoon? I mean to say, I've asked a few of my pals in to meet you, don't you know."

The old boy cocked a speculative eye at him.

"There will be no reporters among them?"

"Reporters? Rather not! Why?"

"I refuse to be badgered by reporters. There were a number of adhesive young men who endeavoured to elicit from me my views on America while the boat was approaching the dock. I will not be subjected to this persecution again."

"That'll be absolutely all right, uncle. There won't be a newspaper-man in the place."

"In that case I shall be glad to make the acquaintance of your friends."

"You'll shake hands with them and so forth?"

"I shall naturally order my behaviour according to the accepted rules of civilized intercourse."

Bicky thanked him heartily and came off to lunch with me at the club, where he babbled freely of hens, incubators, and other rotten things.

After mature consideration we had decided to unleash the Birdsburg contingent on the old boy ten at a time. Jeeves brought his theatre pal round to see us, and we arranged the whole thing with him. A very decent chappie, but rather inclined to collar the conversation and turn it in the direction of his home-town's new water-supply system. We settled that, as an hour was about all he would be likely to stand, each gang should consider itself entitled to seven minutes of the duke's society by Jeeves's stop-watch, and that when their time was up Jeeves should slide into the room and cough meaningly. Then we parted with what I believe are called mutual expressions of goodwill, the Birdsburg chappie extending a cordial invitation to us all to pop out some day and take a look at the new water-supply system, for which we thanked him.

Next day the deputation rolled in. The first shift consisted of the cove we had met and nine others almost exactly like him in every respect. They all looked deuced keen and businesslike, as if from youth up they had been working in the office and catching the boss's eye and what-not. They shook hands with the old boy with a good deal of apparent satisfaction—all except one chappie, who seemed to be brooding about something—and then they stood off and became chatty.

"What message have you for Birdsburg, Duke?" asked our pal.

The old boy seemed a bit rattled.

"I have never been to Birdsburg."

The chappie seemed pained.

"You should pay it a visit," he said. "The most rapidly-growing city in the country. Boost for Birdsburg!"

"Boost for Birdsburg!" said the other chappies reverently.

The chappie who had been brooding suddenly gave tongue.

"Say!"

He was a stout sort of well-fed cove with one of those determined chins and a cold eye.

The assemblage looked at him.

"As a matter of business," said the chappie—"mind you, I'm not questioning anybody's good faith, but, as a matter of strict business—I think this gentleman here ought to put himself on record before witnesses as stating that he really is a duke."

"What do you mean, sir?" cried the old boy, getting purple.

"No offence, simply business. I'm not saying anything, mind you, but there's one thing that seems kind of funny to me. This gentleman here says his name's Mr. Bickersteth, as I understand it. Well, if you're the Duke of Chiswick, why isn't he Lord Percy Something? I've read English novels, and I know all about it."

"This is monstrous!"

"Now don't get hot under the collar. I'm only asking. I've a right to know. You're going to take our money, so it's only fair that we should see that we get our money's worth."

The water-supply cove chipped in:

"You're quite right, Simms. I overlooked that when making the agreement. You see, gentlemen, as business men we've a right to reasonable guarantees of good faith. We are paying Mr. Bickersteth here a hundred and fifty dollars for this reception, and we naturally want to know——"

Old Chiswick gave Bicky a searching look; then he turned to the water-supply chappie. He was frightfully calm.

"I can assure you that I know nothing of this," he said, quite politely. "I should be grateful if you would explain."

"Well, we arranged with Mr. Bickersteth that eighty-seven citizens of Birdsburg should have the privilege of meeting and shaking hands with you for a financial consideration mutually arranged, and what my friend Simms here means—and I'm with him—is that we have only Mr. Bickersteth's word for it—and he is a stranger to us—that you are the Duke of Chiswick at all."

Old Chiswick gulped.

"Allow me to assure you, sir," he said, in a rummy kind of voice, "that I am the Duke of Chiswick."

"Then that's all right," said the chappie heartily. "That was all we wanted to know. Let the thing go on."

"I am sorry to say," said old Chiswick, "that it cannot go on. I am feeling a little tired. I fear I must ask to be excused."

"But there are seventy-seven of the boys waiting round the corner at this moment, Duke, to be introduced to you."

"I fear I must disappoint them."

"But in that case the deal would have to be off."

"That is a matter for you and my nephew to discuss."

The chappie seemed troubled.

"You really won't meet the rest of them?"

"No!"

"Well, then, I guess we'll be going."

They went out, and there was a pretty solid silence. Then old Chiswick turned to Bicky:

"Well?"

Bicky didn't seem to have anything to say.

"Was it true what that man said?"

"Yes, uncle."

"What do you mean by playing this trick?"

Bicky seemed pretty well knocked out, so I put in a word.

"I think you'd better explain the whole thing, Bicky, old top."

Bicky's Adam's-apple jumped about a bit; then he started:

"You see, you had cut off my allowance, uncle, and I wanted a bit of money to start a chicken farm. I mean to say it's an absolute cert if you once get a bit of capital. You buy a hen, and it lays an egg every day of the week, and you sell the eggs, say, seven for twenty-five cents.

"Keep of hens cost nothing. Profit practically——"

"What is all this nonsense about hens? You led me to suppose you were a substantial business man."

"Old Bicky rather exaggerated, sir," I said, helping the chappie out. "The fact is, the poor old lad is absolutely dependent on that remittance of yours, and when you cut it off, don't you know, he was pretty solidly in the soup, and had to think of some way of closing in on a bit of the ready pretty quick. That's why we thought of this handshaking scheme."

Old Chiswick foamed at the mouth.

"So you have lied to me! You have deliberately deceived me as to your financial status!"

"Poor old Bicky didn't want to go to that ranch," I explained. "He doesn't like cows and horses, but he rather thinks he would be hot stuff among the hens. All he wants is a bit of capital. Don't you think it would be rather a wheeze if you were to——"

"After what has happened? After this—this deceit and foolery? Not a penny!"

"But——"

"Not a penny!"

There was a respectful cough in the background.

"If I might make a suggestion, sir?"

Jeeves was standing on the horizon, looking devilish brainy.

"Go ahead, Jeeves!" I said.

"I would merely suggest, sir, that if Mr. Bickersteth is in need of a little ready money, and is at a loss to obtain it elsewhere, he might secure the sum he requires by describing the occurrences of this afternoon for the Sunday issue of one of the more spirited and enterprising newspapers."

"By Jove!" I said.

"By George!" said Bicky.

"Great heavens!" said old Chiswick.

"Very good, sir," said Jeeves.

Bicky turned to old Chiswick with a gleaming eye.

"Jeeves is right. I'll do it! The *Chronicle* would jump at it. They eat that sort of stuff."

Old Chiswick gave a kind of moaning howl.

"I absolutely forbid you, Francis, to do this thing!"

"That's all very well," said Bicky, wonderfully braced, "but if I can't get the money any other way——"

"Wait! Er—wait, my boy! You are so impetuous! We might arrange something."

"I won't go to that bally ranch."

"No, no! No, no, my boy! I would not suggest it. I would not for a moment suggest it. I—I think——"

He seemed to have a bit of a struggle with himself. "I—I think that, on the whole, it would be best if you returned with me to England. I—I might—in fact, I think I see my way to doing—to—I might be able to utilize your services in some secretarial position."

"I shouldn't mind that."

"I should not be able to offer you a salary, but, as you know, in English political life the unpaid secretary is a recognized figure——"

"The only figure I'll recognize," said Bicky firmly, "is five hundred quid a year, paid quarterly."

"My dear boy!"

"Absolutely!"

"But your recompense, my dear Francis, would consist in the unrivalled opportunities you would have, as my secretary, to gain experience, to accustom yourself to the intricacies of political life, to—in fact, you would be in an exceedingly advantageous position."

"Five hundred a year!" said Bicky, rolling it round his tongue. "Why, that would be nothing to what I could make if I started a chicken farm. It stands to reason. Suppose you have a dozen hens. Each of the hens has a dozen chickens. After a bit the chickens grow up and have a dozen chickens each themselves, and then they all start laying eggs! There's a fortune in it. You can get anything you like for eggs in America. Chappies keep them on ice for years and years, and don't sell them till they fetch about a dollar a whirl. You don't think I'm going to chuck a future like this for anything under five hundred o' goblins a year—what?"

A look of anguish passed over old Chiswick's face, then he seemed to be resigned to it. "Very well, my boy," he said.

"What-o!" said Bicky. "All right, then."

"Jeeves," I said. Bicky had taken the old boy off to dinner to celebrate, and we were alone. "Jeeves, this has been one of your best efforts."

"Thank you, sir."

"It beats me how you do it."

"Yes, sir."

"The only trouble is you haven't got much out of it—what!"

"I fancy Mr. Bickersteth intends—I judge from his remarks—to signify his appreciation of anything I have been fortunate enough to do to assist him, at some later date when he is in a more favourable position to do so."

"It isn't enough, Jeeves!"

"Sir?"

It was a wrench, but I felt it was the only possible thing to be done.

"Bring my shaving things."

A gleam of hope shone in the chappie's eye, mixed with doubt.

"You mean, sir?"

"And shave off my moustache."

There was a moment's silence. I could see the fellow was deeply moved.

"Thank you very much indeed, sir," he said, in a low voice, and popped off.

CHAPTER - 4

ABSENT TREATMENT

I want to tell you all about dear old Bobbie Cardew. It's a most interesting story. I can't put in any literary style and all that; but I don't have to, don't you know, because it goes on its Moral Lesson. If you're a man you mustn't miss it, because it'll be a warning to you; and if you're a woman you won't want to, because it's all about how a girl made a man feel pretty well fed up with things.

If you're a recent acquaintance of Bobbie's, you'll probably be surprised to hear that there was a time when he was more remarkable for the weakness of his memory than anything else. Dozens of fellows, who have only met Bobbie since the change took place, have been surprised when I told them that. Yet it's true. Believe me.

In the days when I first knew him Bobbie Cardew was about the most pronounced young rotter inside the four-mile radius. People have called me a silly ass, but I was never in the same class with Bobbie. When it came to being a silly ass, he was a plus-four man, while my handicap was about six. Why, if I wanted him to dine with me, I used to post him a letter at the beginning of the week, and then the day before send him a telegram and a phone-call on the day itself, and—half an hour before the time we'd fixed—a messenger in a taxi, whose business it was to see that he got in and that the chauffeur had the address all correct. By doing this I generally managed to get him, unless he had left town before my messenger arrived.

The funny thing was that he wasn't altogether a fool in other ways. Deep down in him there was a kind of stratum of sense. I had known him, once or twice, show an almost human intelligence. But to reach that stratum, mind you, you needed dynamite.

At least, that's what I thought. But there was another way which hadn't occurred to me. Marriage, I mean. Marriage, the dynamite of the soul; that was what hit Bobbie. He married. Have you ever seen a bull-pup chasing a bee? The pup sees the bee. It looks good to him. But he still doesn't know what's at the end of it till he gets there. It was like that with Bobbie. He fell in love, got married—with a sort of whoop, as if it were the greatest fun in the world—and then began to find out things.

She wasn't the sort of girl you would have expected Bobbie to rave about. And yet, I don't know. What I mean is, she worked for her living; and to a fellow who has never done a hand's turn in his life there's undoubtedly a sort of fascination, a kind of romance, about a girl who works for her living.

Her name was Anthony. Mary Anthony. She was about five feet six; she had a ton and a half of red-gold hair, grey eyes, and one of those determined chins. She was a hospital nurse. When Bobbie smashed himself up at polo, she was told off by the authorities to smooth his brow and rally round with cooling unguents and all that; and the old boy hadn't been up and about again for more than a week before they popped off to the registrar's and fixed it up. Quite the romance.

Bobbie broke the news to me at the club one evening, and next day he introduced me to her. I admired her. I've never worked myself—my name's Pepper, by the way. Almost forgot to mention it. Reggie Pepper. My uncle Edward was Pepper, Wells, and Co., the Colliery people. He left me a sizable chunk of bullion—I say I've never worked myself, but I admire any one who earns a living under difficulties, especially a girl. And this girl had had a rather unusually tough time of it, being an orphan and all that, and having had to do everything off her own bat for years.

Mary and I got along together splendidly. We don't now, but we'll come to that later. I'm speaking of the past. She seemed to think Bobbie the greatest thing on earth, judging by the way she looked at him when she thought I wasn't noticing. And Bobbie seemed to think the same about her. So that I came to the conclusion that, if only dear old Bobbie didn't forget to go to the wedding, they had a sporting chance of being quite happy.

Well, let's brisk up a bit here, and jump a year. The story doesn't really start till then.

They took a flat and settled down. I was in and out of the place quite a good deal. I kept my eyes open, and everything seemed to me to be running along as smoothly as you could want. If this was marriage, I thought, I couldn't see why fellows were so frightened of it. There were a lot of worse things that could happen to a man.

But we now come to the incident of the quiet Dinner, and it's just here that love's young dream hits a snag, and things begin to occur.

I happened to meet Bobbie in Piccadilly, and he asked me to come back to dinner at the flat. And, like a fool, instead of bolting and putting myself under police protection, I went.

When we got to the flat, there was Mrs. Bobbie looking—well, I tell you, it staggered me. Her gold hair was all piled up in waves and crinkles and things, with a what-d'-you-call-it of diamonds in it. And she was wearing the most perfectly ripping dress. I couldn't begin to describe it. I can only say it was the limit. It struck me that if this was how she was in the habit of looking every night when they were dining quietly at home together, it was no wonder that Bobbie liked domesticity.

"Here's old Reggie, dear," said Bobbie. "I've brought him home to have a bit of dinner. I'll phone down to the kitchen and ask them to send it up now—what?"

She stared at him as if she had never seen him before. Then she turned scarlet. Then she turned as white as a sheet. Then she gave a little laugh. It was most interesting to watch. Made me wish I was up a tree about eight hundred miles away. Then she recovered herself.

"I am so glad you were able to come, Mr. Pepper," she said, smiling at me.

And after that she was all right. At least, you would have said so. She talked a lot at dinner, and chaffed Bobbie, and played us ragtime on the piano afterwards, as if she hadn't a care in the world. Quite a jolly little party it was—not. I'm no lynx-eyed sleuth, and all that sort of thing, but I had seen her face at the beginning, and I knew that she was working the whole time and working hard, to keep herself in hand, and that she would have given that diamond what's-its-name in her hair and everything else she possessed to have one good scream—just one. I've sat through some pretty thick evenings in my time, but that one had the rest beaten in a canter. At the very earliest moment I grabbed my hat and got away.

Having seen what I did, I wasn't particularly surprised to meet Bobbie at the club next day looking about as merry and bright as a lonely gum-drop at an Eskimo tea-party.

He started in straightway. He seemed glad to have someone to talk to about it.

"Do you know how long I've been married?" he said.

I didn't exactly.

"About a year, isn't it?"

"Not *about* a year," he said sadly. "Exactly a year—yesterday!"

Then I understood. I saw light—a regular flash of light.

"Yesterday was——?"

"The anniversary of the wedding. I'd arranged to take Mary to the Savoy, and on to Covent Garden. She particularly wanted to hear Caruso. I had the ticket for the box in my pocket. Do you know, all through dinner I had a kind of rummy idea that there was something I'd forgotten, but I couldn't think what?"

"Till your wife mentioned it?"

He nodded——

"She—mentioned it," he said thoughtfully.

I didn't ask for details. Women with hair and chins like Mary's may be angels most of the time, but, when they take off their wings for a bit, they aren't half-hearted about it.

"To be absolutely frank, old top," said poor old Bobbie, in a broken sort of way, "my stock's pretty low at home."

There didn't seem much to be done. I just lit a cigarette and sat there. He didn't want to talk. Presently he went out. I stood at the window of our upper smoking-room, which looks out on to Piccadilly, and watched him. He walked slowly along for a few yards, stopped, then walked on again, and finally turned into a jeweller's. Which was an instance of what I meant when I said that deep down in him there was a certain stratum of sense.

It was from now on that I began to be really interested in this problem of Bobbie's married life. Of course, one's always mildly interested in one's friends' marriages, hoping they'll turn out well and all that; but this was different. The average man isn't like Bobbie, and the average girl isn't like Mary. It was that old business of the immovable mass and the irresistible force. There was Bobbie, ambling gently through life, a dear old chap in a hundred ways, but undoubtedly a chump of the first water.

And there was Mary, determined that he shouldn't be a chump. And Nature, mind you, on Bobbie's side. When Nature makes a chump like dear old Bobbie, she's proud of him, and doesn't want her handiwork disturbed. She gives him a sort of natural armour to protect him against outside interference. And that armour is shortness of memory. Shortness of memory keeps a man a chump, when, but for it, he might cease to be one. Take my case, for instance. I'm a chump. Well, if I had remembered half the things people have tried to teach me during my life, my size in hats would be about number nine. But I didn't. I forgot them. And it was just the same with Bobbie.

For about a week, perhaps a bit more, the recollection of that quiet little domestic evening bucked him up like a tonic. Elephants, I read somewhere, are champions at the memory business, but they were fools to Bobbie during that week. But, bless you, the shock wasn't nearly big enough. It had dinted the armour, but it hadn't made a hole in it. Pretty soon he was back at the old game.

It was pathetic, don't you know. The poor girl loved him, and she was frightened. It was the thin edge of the wedge, you see, and she knew it. A man who forgets what day he was married, when he's been married one year, will forget, at about the end of the fourth, that he's married at all. If she meant to get him in hand at all, she had got to do it now, before he began to drift away.

I saw that clearly enough, and I tried to make Bobbie see it, when he was by way of pouring out his troubles to me one afternoon. I can't remember what it was that he had forgotten the day before, but it was something she had asked him to bring home for her—it may have been a book.

"It's such a little thing to make a fuss about," said Bobbie. "And she knows that it's simply because I've got such an infernal memory about everything. I can't remember anything. Never could."

He talked on for a while, and, just as he was going, he pulled out a couple of sovereigns.

"Oh, by the way," he said.

"What's this for?" I asked, though I knew.

"I owe it you."

"How's that?" I said.

"Why, that bet on Tuesday. In the billiard-room. Murray and Brown were playing a hundred up, and I gave you two to one that Brown would win, and Murray beat him by twenty odd."

"So you do remember some things?" I said.

He got quite excited. Said that if I thought he was the sort of rotter who forgot to pay when he lost a bet, it was pretty rotten of me after knowing him all these years, and a lot more like that.

"Subside, laddie," I said.

Then I spoke to him like a father.

"What you've got to do, my old college chum," I said, "is to pull yourself together, and jolly quick, too. As things are shaping, you're due for a nasty knock before you know what's hit you. You've got to make an effort. Don't say you can't. This two quid business shows that, even if your memory is rocky, you can remember some things. What you've got to do is to see that wedding anniversaries and so on are included in the list. It may be a brainstrain, but you can't get out of it."

"I suppose you're right," said Bobbie. "But it beats me why she thinks such a lot of these rotten little dates. What's it matter if I forgot what day we were married on or what day she was born on or what day the cat had the measles? She knows I love her just as much as if I were a memorizing freak at the halls."

"That's not enough for a woman," I said. "They want to be shown. Bear that in mind, and you're all right. Forget it, and there'll be trouble."

He chewed the knob of his stick.

"Women are frightfully rummy," he said gloomily.

"You should have thought of that before you married one," I said.

I don't see that I could have done any more. I had put the whole thing in a nutshell for him. You would have thought he'd have seen the point, and that it would have made him brace up and get a hold on himself. But no. Off he went again in the same old way. I gave up arguing with him. I had a good deal of time on my hands, but not enough to amount to anything when it was a question of reforming dear old Bobbie by argument. If you see a man asking for trouble, and insisting on getting it, the only thing to do is to stand by and wait till it comes to him. After that you may get a chance. But till then there's nothing to be done. But I thought a lot about him.

Bobbie didn't get into the soup all at once. Weeks went by, and months, and still nothing happened. Now and then he'd come into the club with a kind of cloud on his shining morning face, and I'd know that there had been doings in the home; but it wasn't till well on in the spring that he got the thunderbolt just where he had been asking for it—in the thorax.

I was smoking a quiet cigarette one morning in the window looking out over Piccadilly, and watching the buses and motors going up one way and down the other—most interesting it is; I often do it—when in rushed Bobbie, with his eyes bulging and his face the colour of an oyster, waving a piece of paper in his hand.

"Reggie," he said. "Reggie, old top, she's gone!"

"Gone!" I said. "Who?"

"Mary, of course! Gone! Left me! Gone!"

"Where?" I said.

Silly question? Perhaps you're right. Anyhow, dear old Bobbie nearly foamed at the mouth.

"Where? How should I know where? Here, read this."

He pushed the paper into my hand. It was a letter.

"Go on," said Bobbie. "Read it."

So I did. It certainly was quite a letter. There was not much of it, but it was all to the point. This is what it said:

"MY DEAR BOBBIE,—I am going away. When you care enough about me to remember to wish me many happy returns on my birthday, I will come back. My address will be Box 341, *London Morning News*."

I read it twice, then I said, "Well, why don't you?"

"Why don't I what?"

"Why don't you wish her many happy returns? It doesn't seem much to ask."

"But she says on her birthday."

"Well, when is her birthday?"

"Can't you understand?" said Bobbie. "I've forgotten."

"Forgotten!" I said.

"Yes," said Bobbie. "Forgotten."

"How do you mean, forgotten?" I said. "Forgotten whether it's the twentieth or the twenty-first, or what? How near do you get to it?"

"I know it came somewhere between the first of January and the thirty-first of December. That's how near I get to it."

"Think."

"Think? What's the use of saying 'Think'? Think I haven't thought? I've been knocking sparks out of my brain ever since I opened that letter."

"And you can't remember?"

"No."

I rang the bell and ordered restoratives.

"Well, Bobbie," I said, "it's a pretty hard case to spring on an untrained amateur like me. Suppose someone had come to Sherlock Holmes and said, 'Mr. Holmes, here's a case for you. When is my wife's birthday?' Wouldn't that have given Sherlock a jolt? However, I know enough about the game to understand that a fellow can't shoot off his deductive theories unless you start him with a clue, so rouse yourself out of that pop-eyed trance and come across with two or three. For instance, can't you remember the last time she had a birthday? What sort of weather was it? That might fix the month."

Bobbie shook his head.

"It was just ordinary weather, as near as I can recollect."

"Warm?"

"Warmish."

"Or cold?"

"Well, fairly cold, perhaps. I can't remember."

I ordered two more of the same. They seemed indicated in the Young Detective's Manual. "You're a great help, Bobbie," I said. "An invaluable assistant. One of those indispensable adjuncts without which no home is complete."

Bobbie seemed to be thinking.

"I've got it," he said suddenly. "Look here. I gave her a present on her last birthday. All we have to do is to go to the shop, hunt up the date when it was bought, and the thing's done."

"Absolutely. What did you give her?"

He sagged.

"I can't remember," he said.

Getting ideas is like golf. Some days you're right off, others it's as easy as falling off a log. I don't suppose dear old Bobbie had ever had two ideas in the same morning before in his life; but now he did it without an effort. He just loosed another dry Martini into the undergrowth, and before you could turn round it had flushed quite a brain-wave.

Do you know those little books called *When were you Born*? There's one for each month. They tell you your character, your talents, your strong points, and your weak points at fourpence halfpenny a go. Bobbie's idea was to buy the whole twelve, and go through them till we found out which month hit off Mary's character. That would give us the month, and narrow it down a whole lot.

A pretty hot idea for a non-thinker like dear old Bobbie. We sallied out at once. He took half and I took half, and we settled down to work. As I say, it sounded good. But when we came to go into the thing, we saw that there was a flaw. There was plenty of information all right, but there wasn't a single month that didn't have something that exactly hit off Mary. For instance, in the December book it said, "December people are apt to keep their own secrets. They are extensive travellers." Well, Mary had certainly kept her secret, and she had travelled quite extensively enough for Bobbie's needs. Then, October people were "born with original ideas" and "loved moving." You couldn't have summed up Mary's little jaunt more neatly. February people had "wonderful memories"—Mary's speciality.

We took a bit of a rest, then had another go at the thing.

Bobbie was all for May, because the book said that women born in that month were "inclined to be capricious, which is always a barrier to a happy married life"; but I plumped for February, because February women "are unusually determined to have their own way, are very earnest, and expect a full return in their companion or mates." Which he owned was about as like Mary as anything could be.

In the end he tore the books up, stamped on them, burnt them, and went home.

It was wonderful what a change the next few days made in dear old Bobbie. Have you ever seen that picture, "The Soul's Awakening"? It represents a flapper of sorts gazing in a startled sort of way into the middle distance with a look in her eyes that seems to say, "Surely that is George's step I hear on the mat! Can this be love?" Well, Bobbie had a soul's awakening too. I don't suppose he had ever troubled to think in his life before—not really *think*. But now he was wearing his brain to the bone. It was painful in a way, of course, to see a fellow human being so thoroughly in the soup, but I felt strongly that it was all for the best. I could see as plainly as possible that all these brainstorms were improving Bobbie out of knowledge. When it was all over he might possibly become a rotter again of a sort, but it would only be a pale reflection of the rotter he had been. It bore out the idea I had always had that what he needed was a real good jolt.

I saw a great deal of him these days. I was his best friend, and he came to me for sympathy. I gave it him, too, with both hands, but I never failed to hand him the Moral Lesson when I had him weak.

One day he came to me as I was sitting in the club, and I could see that he had had an idea. He looked happier than he had done in weeks.

"Reggie," he said, "I'm on the trail. This time I'm convinced that I shall pull it off. I've remembered something of vital importance."

"Yes?" I said.

"I remember distinctly," he said, "that on Mary's last birthday we went together to the Coliseum. How does that hit you?"

"It's a fine bit of memorizing," I said; "but how does it help?"

"Why, they change the programme every week there."

"Ah!" I said. "Now you are talking."

"And the week we went one of the turns was Professor Some One's Terpsichorean Cats. I recollect them distinctly. Now, are we narrowing it down, or aren't we? Reggie, I'm going round to the Coliseum this minute, and I'm going to dig the date of those Terpsichorean Cats out of them, if I have to use a crowbar."

So that got him within six days; for the management treated us like brothers; brought out the archives, and ran agile fingers over the pages till they treed the cats in the middle of May.

"I told you it was May," said Bobbie. "Maybe you'll listen to me another time."

"If you've any sense," I said, "there won't be another time."

And Bobbie said that there wouldn't.

Once you get your memory on the run, it parts as if it enjoyed doing it. I had just got off to sleep that night when my telephone-bell rang. It was Bobbie, of course. He didn't apologize.

"Reggie," he said, "I've got it now for certain. It's just come to me. We saw those Terpsichorean Cats at a matinee, old man."

"Yes?" I said.

"Well, don't you see that that brings it down to two days? It must have been either Wednesday the seventh or Saturday the tenth."

"Yes," I said, "if they didn't have daily matinees at the Coliseum."

I heard him give a sort of howl.

"Bobbie," I said. My feet were freezing, but I was fond of him.

"Well?"

"I've remembered something too. It's this. The day you went to the Coliseum I lunched with you both at the Ritz. You had forgotten to bring any money with you, so you wrote a cheque."

"But I'm always writing cheques."

"You are. But this was for a tenner, and made out to the hotel. Hunt up your cheque-book and see how many cheques for ten pounds payable to the Ritz Hotel you wrote out between May the fifth and May the tenth."

He gave a kind of gulp.

"Reggie," he said, "you're a genius. I've always said so. I believe you've got it. Hold the line."

Presently he came back again.

"Halloa!" he said.

"I'm here," I said.

"It was the eighth. Reggie, old man, I——"

"Topping," I said. "Good night."

It was working along into the small hours now, but I thought I might as well make a night of it and finish the thing up, so I rang up an hotel near the Strand.

"Put me through to Mrs. Cardew," I said.

"It's late," said the man at the other end.

"And getting later every minute," I said. "Buck along, laddie."

I waited patiently. I had missed my beauty-sleep, and my feet had frozen hard, but I was past regrets.

"What is the matter?" said Mary's voice.

"My feet are cold," I said. "But I didn't call you up to tell you that particularly. I've just been chatting with Bobbie, Mrs. Cardew."

"Oh! is that Mr. Pepper?"

"Yes. He's remembered it, Mrs. Cardew."

She gave a sort of scream. I've often thought how interesting it must be to be one of those Exchange girls. The things they must hear, don't you know. Bobbie's howl and gulp and Mrs. Bobbie's scream and all about my feet and all that. Most interesting it must be.

"He's remembered it!" she gasped. "Did you tell him?"

"No."

Well, I hadn't.

"Mr. Pepper."

"Yes?"

"Was he—has he been—was he very worried?"

I chuckled. This was where I was billed to be the life and soul of the party.

"Worried! He was about the most worried man between here and Edinburgh. He has been worrying as if he was paid to do it by the nation. He has started out to worry after breakfast, and——"

Oh, well, you can never tell with women. My idea was that we should pass the rest of the night slapping each other on the back across the wire, and telling each other what bally brainy conspirators we were, don't you know, and all that. But I'd got just as far as this, when she bit at me. Absolutely! I heard the snap. And then she said "Oh!" in that choked kind of way. And when a woman says "Oh!" like that, it means all the bad words she'd love to say if she only knew them.

And then she began.

"What brutes men are! What horrid brutes! How you could stand by and see poor dear Bobbie worrying himself into a fever, when a word from you would have put everything right, I can't——"

"But——"

"And you call yourself his friend! His friend!" (Metallic laugh, most unpleasant.) "It shows how one can be deceived. I used to think you a kind-hearted man."

"But, I say, when I suggested the thing, you thought it perfectly——"

"I thought it hateful, abominable."

"But you said it was absolutely top——"

"I said nothing of the kind. And if I did, I didn't mean it. I don't wish to be unjust, Mr. Pepper, but I must say that to me there seems to be something positively fiendish in a man who can go out of his way to separate a husband from his wife, simply in order to amuse himself by gloating over his agony—

"But——!"

"When one single word would have——"

"But you made me promise not to——" I bleated.

"And if I did, do you suppose I didn't expect you to have the sense to break your promise?"

I had finished. I had no further observations to make. I hung up the receiver, and crawled into bed.

I still see Bobbie when he comes to the club, but I do not visit the old homestead. He is friendly, but he stops short of issuing invitations. I ran across Mary at the Academy last week, and her eyes went through me like a couple of bullets through a pat of butter. And as they came out the other side, and I limped off to piece myself together again, there occurred to me the simple epitaph which, when I am no more, I intend to have inscribed on my tombstone. It was this: "He was a man who acted from the best motives. There is one born every minute."

Chapter - 5

HELPING FREDDIE

I don't want to bore you, don't you know, and all that sort of rot, but I must tell you about dear old Freddie Meadowes. I'm not a flier at literary style, and all that, but I'll get some writer chappie to give the thing a wash and brush up when I've finished, so that'll be all right.

Dear old Freddie, don't you know, has been a dear old pal of mine for years and years; so when I went into the club one morning and found him sitting alone in a dark corner, staring glassily at nothing, and generally looking like the last rose of summer, you can understand I was quite disturbed about it. As a rule, the old rotter is the life and soul of our set. Quite the little lump of fun, and all that sort of thing.

Jimmy Pinkerton was with me at the time. Jimmy's a fellow who writes plays—a deuced brainy sort of fellow—and between us we set to work to question the poor pop-eyed chappie, until finally we got at what the matter was.

As we might have guessed, it was a girl. He had had a quarrel with Angela West, the girl he was engaged to, and she had broken off the engagement. What the row had been about he didn't say, but apparently she was pretty well fed up. She wouldn't let him come near her, refused to talk on the phone, and sent back his letters unopened.

I was sorry for poor old Freddie. I knew what it felt like. I was once in love myself with a girl called Elizabeth Shoolbred, and the fact that she couldn't stand me at any price will be recorded in my autobiography. I knew the thing for Freddie.

"Change of scene is what you want, old scout," I said. "Come with me to Marvis Bay. I've taken a cottage there. Jimmy's coming down on the twenty-fourth. We'll be a cosy party."

"He's absolutely right," said Jimmy. "Change of scene's the thing. I knew a man. Girl refused him. Man went abroad. Two months later girl wired him, 'Come back. Muriel.' Man started to write out a reply; suddenly found that he couldn't remember girl's surname; so never answered at all."

But Freddie wouldn't be comforted. He just went on looking as if he had swallowed his last sixpence. However, I got him to promise to come to Marvis Bay with me. He said he might as well be there as anywhere.

Do you know Marvis Bay? It's in Dorsetshire. It isn't what you'd call a fiercely exciting spot, but it has its good points. You spend the day there bathing and sitting on the sands, and in the evening you stroll out on the shore with the gnats. At nine o'clock you rub ointment on the wounds and go to bed.

It seemed to suit poor old Freddie. Once the moon was up and the breeze sighing in the trees, you couldn't drag him from that beach with a rope. He became quite a popular pet with the gnats. They'd hang round waiting for him to come out, and would give perfectly good strollers the miss-in-baulk just so as to be in good condition for him.

Yes, it was a peaceful sort of life, but by the end of the first week I began to wish that Jimmy Pinkerton had arranged to come down earlier: for as a companion Freddie, poor old chap, wasn't anything to write home to mother about. When he wasn't chewing a pipe and scowling at the carpet, he was sitting at the piano, playing "The Rosary" with one finger. He couldn't play anything except "The Rosary," and he couldn't play much of that. Somewhere round about the third bar a fuse would blow out, and he'd have to start all over again.

He was playing it as usual one morning when I came in from bathing.

"Reggie," he said, in a hollow voice, looking up, "I've seen her."

"Seen her?" I said. "What, Miss West?"

"I was down at the post office, getting the letters, and we met in the doorway. She cut me!"

He started "The Rosary" again, and side-slipped in the second bar.

"Reggie," he said, "you ought never to have brought me here. I must go away."

"Go away?" I said. "Don't talk such rot. This is the best thing that could have happened. This is where you come out strong."

"She cut me."

"Never mind. Be a sportsman. Have another dash at her."

"She looked clean through me!"

"Of course she did. But don't mind that. Put this thing in my hands. I'll see you through. Now, what you want," I said, "is to place her under some obligation to you. What you want is to get her timidly thanking you. What you want——"

"But what's she going to thank me timidly for?"

I thought for a moment.

"Look out for a chance and save her from drowning," I said.

"I can't swim," said Freddie.

That was Freddie all over, don't you know. A dear old chap in a thousand ways, but no help to a fellow, if you know what I mean.

He cranked up the piano once more and I sprinted for the open.

I strolled out on to the sands and began to think this thing over. There was no doubt that the brain-work had got to be done by me. Dear old Freddie had his strong qualities. He was top-hole at polo, and in happier days I've heard him give an imitation of cats fighting in a backyard that would have surprised you. But apart from that he wasn't a man of enterprise.

Well, don't you know, I was rounding some rocks, with my brain whirring like a dynamo, when I caught sight of a blue dress, and, by Jove, it was the girl. I had never met her, but Freddie had sixteen photographs of her sprinkled round his bedroom, and I knew I couldn't be mistaken. She was sitting on the sand, helping a small, fat child build a castle. On a chair close by was an elderly lady reading a novel. I heard the girl call her "aunt." So, doing the Sherlock Holmes business, I deduced that the fat child was her cousin. It struck me that if Freddie had been there he would probably have tried to work up some sentiment about the kid on the strength of it. Personally I couldn't manage it. I don't think I ever saw a child who made me feel less sentimental. He was one of those round, bulging kids.

After he had finished the castle he seemed to get bored with life, and began to whimper. The girl took him off to where a fellow was selling sweets at a stall. And I walked on.

Now, fellows, if you ask them, will tell you that I'm a chump. Well, I don't mind. I admit it. I *am* a chump. All the Peppers have been chumps. But what I do say is that every now and then, when you'd least expect it, I get a pretty hot brain-wave; and that's what happened now. I doubt if the idea that came to me then would have occurred to a single one of any dozen of the brainiest chappies you care to name.

It came to me on my return journey. I was walking back along the shore, when I saw the fat kid meditatively smacking a jelly-fish with a spade. The girl wasn't with him. In fact, there didn't seem to be any one in sight. I was just going to pass on when I got the brain-wave. I thought the whole thing out in a flash, don't you know. From what I had seen of the two, the girl was evidently fond of this kid, and, anyhow, he was her cousin, so what I said to myself was this: If I kidnap this young heavy-weight for the moment, and if, when the girl has got frightfully anxious about where he can have got to, dear old Freddie suddenly appears leading the infant by the hand and telling a story to the effect that he has found him wandering at large about the country and practically saved his life, why, the girl's gratitude is bound to make her chuck hostilities and be friends again. So I gathered in the kid and made off with him. All the way home I pictured that scene of reconciliation. I could see it so vividly, don't you know, that, by George, it gave me quite a choky feeling in my throat.

Freddie, dear old chap, was rather slow at getting on to the fine points of the idea. When I appeared, carrying the kid, and dumped him down in our sitting-room, he didn't absolutely effervesce with joy, if you know what I mean. The kid had started to bellow by this time, and poor old Freddie seemed to find it rather trying.

"Stop it!" he said. "Do you think nobody's got any troubles except you? What the deuce is all this, Reggie?"

The kid came back at him with a yell that made the window rattle. I raced to the kitchen and fetched a jar of honey. It was the right stuff. The kid stopped bellowing and began to smear his face with the stuff.

"Well?" said Freddie, when silence had set in. I explained the idea. After a while it began to strike him.

"You're not such a fool as you look, sometimes, Reggie," he said handsomely. "I'm bound to say this seems pretty good."

And he disentangled the kid from the honey-jar and took him out, to scour the beach for Angela.

I don't know when I've felt so happy. I was so fond of dear old Freddie that to know that he was soon going to be his old bright self again made me feel as if somebody had left me about a million pounds. I was leaning back in a chair on the veranda, smoking peacefully, when down the road I saw the old boy returning, and, by George, the kid was still with him. And Freddie looked as if he hadn't a friend in the world.

"Hello!" I said. "Couldn't you find her?"

"Yes, I found her," he replied, with one of those bitter, hollow laughs.

"Well, then——?"

Freddie sank into a chair and groaned.

"This isn't her cousin, you idiot!" he said.

"He's no relation at all. He's just a kid she happened to meet on the beach. She had never seen him before in her life."

"What! Who is he, then?"

"I don't know. Oh, Lord, I've had a time! Thank goodness you'll probably spend the next few years of your life in Dartmoor for kidnapping. That's my only consolation. I'll come and jeer at you through the bars."

"Tell me all, old boy," I said.

It took him a good long time to tell the story, for he broke off in the middle of nearly every sentence to call me names, but I gathered gradually what had happened. She had listened like an iceberg while he told the story he had prepared, and then—well, she didn't actually call him a liar, but she gave him to understand in a general sort of way that if he and Dr. Cook ever happened to meet, and started swapping stories, it would be about the biggest duel on record. And then he had crawled away with the kid, licked to a splinter.

"And mind, this is your affair," he concluded. "I'm not mixed up in it at all. If you want to escape your sentence, you'd better go and find the kid's parents and return him before the police come for you."

By Jove, you know, till I started to tramp the place with this infernal kid, I never had a notion it would have been so deuced difficult to restore a child to its anxious parents. It's a mystery to me how kidnappers ever get caught. I searched Marvis Bay like a bloodhound, but nobody came forward to claim the infant. You'd have thought, from the lack of interest in him, that he was stopping there all by himself in a cottage of his own. It wasn't till, by an inspiration, I thought to ask the sweet-stall man that I found out that his name was Medwin, and that his parents lived at a place called Ocean Rest, in Beach Road.

I shot off there like an arrow and knocked at the door. Nobody answered. I knocked again. I could hear movements inside, but nobody came. I was just going to get to work on that knocker in such a way that the idea would filter through into these people's heads that I wasn't standing there just for the fun of the thing, when a voice from somewhere above shouted, "Hi!"

I looked up and saw a round, pink face, with grey whiskers east and west of it, staring down from an upper window.

"Hi!" it shouted again.

"What the deuce do you mean by 'Hi'?" I said.

"You can't come in," said the face. "Hello, is that Tootles?"

"My name is not Tootles, and I don't want to come in," I said. "Are you Mr. Medwin? I've brought back your son."

"I see him. Peep-bo, Tootles! Dadda can see 'oo!"

The face disappeared with a jerk. I could hear voices. The face reappeared.

"Hi!"

I churned the gravel madly.

"Do you live here?" said the face.

"I'm staying here for a few weeks."

"What's your name?"

"Pepper. But——"

"Pepper? Any relation to Edward Pepper, the colliery owner?"

"My uncle. But——"

"I used to know him well. Dear old Edward Pepper! I wish I was with him now."

"I wish you were," I said.

He beamed down at me.

"This is most fortunate," he said. "We were wondering what we were to do with Tootles. You see, we have the mumps here. My daughter Bootles has just developed mumps. Tootles must not be exposed to the risk of infection. We could not think what we were to do with him. It was most fortunate your finding him. He strayed from his nurse. I would hesitate to trust him to the care of a stranger, but you are different. Any nephew of Edward Pepper's has my implicit confidence. You must take Tootles to your house. It will be an ideal arrangement. I have written to my brother in London to come and fetch him. He may be here in a few days."

"May!"

"He is a busy man, of course; but he should certainly be here within a week. Till then Tootles can stop with you. It is an excellent plan. Very much obliged to you. Your wife will like Tootles."

"I haven't got a wife," I yelled; but the window had closed with a bang, as if the man with the whiskers had found a germ trying to escape, don't you know, and had headed it off just in time.

I breathed a deep breath and wiped my forehead.

The window flew up again.

"Hi!"

A package weighing about a ton hit me on the head and burst like a bomb.

"Did you catch it?" said the face, reappearing. "Dear me, you missed it! Never mind. You can get it at the grocer's. Ask for Bailey's Granulated Breakfast Chips. Tootles takes them for breakfast with a little milk. Be certain to get Bailey's."

My spirit was broken, if you know what I mean. I accepted the situation. Taking Tootles by the hand, I walked slowly away. Napoleon's retreat from Moscow was a picnic by the side of it.

As we turned up the road we met Freddie's Angela.

The sight of her had a marked effect on the kid Tootles. He pointed at her and said, "Wah!"

The girl stopped and smiled. I loosed the kid, and he ran to her.

"Well, baby?" she said, bending down to him. "So father found you again, did he? Your little son and I made friends on the beach this morning," she said to me.

This was the limit. Coming on top of that interview with the whiskered lunatic it so utterly unnerved me, don't you know, that she had nodded good-bye and was half-way down the road before I caught up with my breath enough to deny the charge of being the infant's father.

I hadn't expected dear old Freddie to sing with joy when he found out what had happened, but I did think he might have shown a little more manly fortitude. He leaped up, glared at the kid, and clutched his head. He didn't speak for a long time, but, on the other hand, when he began he did not leave off for a long time. He was quite emotional, dear old boy. It beat me where he could have picked up such expressions.

"Well," he said, when he had finished, "say something! Heavens! man, why don't you say something?"

"You don't give me a chance, old top," I said soothingly.

"What are you going to do about it?"

"What can we do about it?"

"We can't spend our time acting as nurses to this—this exhibit."

He got up.

"I'm going back to London," he said.

"Freddie!" I cried. "Freddie, old man!" My voice shook. "Would you desert a pal at a time like this?"

"I would. This is your business, and you've got to manage it."

"Freddie," I said, "you've got to stand by me. You must. Do you realize that this child has to be undressed, and bathed, and dressed again? You wouldn't leave me to do all that single-handed? Freddie, old scout, we were at school together. Your mother likes me. You owe me a tenner."

He sat down again.

"Oh, well," he said resignedly.

"Besides, old top," I said, "I did it all for your sake, don't you know?"

He looked at me in a curious way.

"Reggie," he said, in a strained voice, "one moment. I'll stand a good deal, but I won't stand for being expected to be grateful."

Looking back at it, I see that what saved me from Colney Hatch in that crisis was my bright idea of buying up most of the contents of the local sweet-shop. By serving out sweets to the kid practically incessantly we managed to get through the rest of that day pretty satisfactorily. At eight o'clock he fell asleep in a chair, and, having undressed him by unbuttoning every button in sight and, where there were no buttons, pulling till something gave, we carried him up to bed.

Freddie stood looking at the pile of clothes on the floor and I knew what he was thinking. To get the kid undressed had been simple—a mere matter of muscle. But how were we to get him into his clothes again? I stirred the pile with my foot. There was a long linen arrangement which might have been anything. Also a strip of pink flannel which was like nothing on earth. We looked at each other and smiled wanly.

But in the morning I remembered that there were children at the next bungalow but one. We went there before breakfast and borrowed their nurse. Women are wonderful, by George they are! She had that kid dressed and looking fit for anything in about eight minutes. I showered wealth on her, and she promised to come in morning and evening. I sat down to breakfast almost cheerful again. It was the first bit of silver lining there had been to the cloud up to date.

"And after all," I said, "there's lots to be said for having a child about the house, if you know what I mean. Kind of cosy and domestic—what!"

Just then the kid upset the milk over Freddie's trousers, and when he had come back after changing his clothes he began to talk about what a much-maligned man King Herod was. The more he saw of Tootles, he said, the less he wondered at those impulsive views of his on infanticide.

Two days later Jimmy Pinkerton came down. Jimmy took one look at the kid, who happened to be howling at the moment, and picked up his portmanteau.

"For me," he said, "the hotel. I can't write dialogue with that sort of thing going on. Whose work is this? Which of you adopted this little treasure?"

I told him about Mr. Medwin and the mumps. Jimmy seemed interested.

"I might work this up for the stage," he said. "It wouldn't make a bad situation for act two of a farce."

"Farce!" snarled poor old Freddie.

"Rather. Curtain of act one on hero, a well-meaning, half-baked sort of idiot just like—that is to say, a well-meaning, half-baked sort of idiot, kidnapping the child. Second act, his adventures with it. I'll rough it out to-night. Come along and show me the hotel, Reggie."

As we went I told him the rest of the story—the Angela part. He laid down his portmanteau and looked at me like an owl through his glasses.

"What!" he said. "Why, hang it, this is a play, ready-made. It's the old 'Tiny Hand' business. Always safe stuff. Parted lovers. Lisping child. Reconciliation over the little cradle. It's big. Child, centre. Girl L.C.; Freddie, up stage, by the piano. Can Freddie play the piano?"

"He can play a little of 'The Rosary' with one finger."

Jimmy shook his head.

"No; we shall have to cut out the soft music. But the rest's all right. Look here." He squatted in the sand. "This stone is the girl. This bit of seaweed's the child. This nutshell is Freddie. Dialogue leading up to child's line. Child speaks like, 'Boofer lady, does 'oo love dadda?' Business of outstretched hands. Hold picture for a moment. Freddie crosses L., takes girl's hand. Business of swallowing lump in throat. Then big speech. 'Ah, Marie,' or whatever her name is—Jane—Agnes—Angela? Very well. 'Ah, Angela, has not this gone on too long? A little child rebukes us! Angela!' And so on. Freddie must work up his own part. I'm just giving you the general outline. And we must get a good line for the child. 'Boofer lady, does 'oo love dadda?' isn't definite enough. We want something more—ah! 'Kiss Freddie,' that's it. Short, crisp, and has the punch."

"But, Jimmy, old top," I said, "the only objection is, don't you know, that there's no way of getting the girl to the cottage. She cuts Freddie. She wouldn't come within a mile of him."

Jimmy frowned.

"That's awkward," he said. "Well, we shall have to make it an exterior set instead of an interior. We can easily corner her on the beach somewhere, when we're ready. Meanwhile, we must get the kid letter-perfect. First rehearsal for lines and business eleven sharp to-morrow."

Poor old Freddie was in such a gloomy state of mind that we decided not to tell him the idea till we had finished coaching the kid. He wasn't in the mood to have a thing like that hanging over him. So we concentrated on Tootles. And pretty early in the proceedings we saw that the only way to get Tootles worked up to the spirit of the thing was to introduce sweets of some sort as a sub-motive, so to speak.

"The chief difficulty," said Jimmy Pinkerton at the end of the first rehearsal, "is to establish a connection in the kid's mind between his line and the sweets. Once he has grasped the basic fact that those two words, clearly spoken, result automatically in acid-drops, we have got a success."

I've often thought, don't you know, how interesting it must be to be one of those animal-trainer Johnnies: to stimulate the dawning intelligence, and that sort of thing. Well, this was every bit as exciting. Some days success seemed to be staring us in the eye, and the kid got the line out as if he'd been an old professional. And then he'd go all to pieces again. And time was flying.

"We must hurry up, Jimmy," I said. "The kid's uncle may arrive any day now and take him away."

"And we haven't an understudy," said Jimmy. "There's something in that. We must work! My goodness, that kid's a bad study. I've known deaf-mutes who would have learned the part quicker."

I will say this for the kid, though: he was a trier. Failure didn't discourage him. Whenever there was any kind of sweet near he had a dash at his line, and kept on saying something till he got what he was after. His only fault was his uncertainty. Personally, I would have been prepared to risk it, and start the performance at the first opportunity, but Jimmy said no.

"We're not nearly ready," said Jimmy. "To-day, for instance, he said 'Kick Freddie.' That's not going to win any girl's heart. And she might do it, too. No; we must postpone production awhile yet."

But, by George, we didn't. The curtain went up the very next afternoon.

It was nobody's fault—certainly not mine. It was just Fate. Freddie had settled down at the piano, and I was leading the kid out of the house to exercise it, when, just as we'd got out to the veranda, along came the girl Angela on her way to the beach. The kid set up his usual yell at the sight of her, and she stopped at the foot of the steps.

"Hello, baby!" she said. "Good morning," she said to me. "May I come up?"

She didn't wait for an answer. She just came. She seemed to be that sort of girl. She came up on the veranda and started fussing over the kid. And six feet away, mind you, Freddie smiting the piano in the sitting-room. It was a dash disturbing situation, don't you know. At any minute Freddie might take it into his head to come out on to the veranda, and we hadn't even begun to rehearse him in his part.

I tried to break up the scene.

"We were just going down to the beach," I said.

"Yes?" said the girl. She listened for a moment. "So you're having your piano tuned?" she said. "My aunt has been trying to find a tuner for ours. Do you mind if I go in and tell this man to come on to us when he's finished here?"

"Er—not yet!" I said. "Not yet, if you don't mind. He can't bear to be disturbed when he's working. It's the artistic temperament. I'll tell him later."

"Very well," she said, getting up to go. "Ask him to call at Pine Bungalow. West is the name. Oh, he seems to have stopped. I suppose he will be out in a minute now. I'll wait."

"Don't you think—shouldn't we be going on to the beach?" I said.

She had started talking to the kid and didn't hear. She was feeling in her pocket for something.

"The beach," I babbled.

"See what I've brought for you, baby," she said. And, by George, don't you know, she held up in front of the kid's bulging eyes a chunk of toffee about the size of the Automobile Club.

That finished it. We had just been having a long rehearsal, and the kid was all worked up in his part. He got it right first time.

"Kiss Fweddie!" he shouted.

And the front door opened, and Freddie came out on to the veranda, for all the world as if he had been taking a cue.

He looked at the girl, and the girl looked at him. I looked at the ground, and the kid looked at the toffee.

"Kiss Fweddie!" he yelled. "Kiss Fweddie!"

The girl was still holding up the toffee, and the kid did what Jimmy Pinkerton would have called "business of outstretched hands" towards it.

"Kiss Fweddie!" he shrieked.

"What does this mean?" said the girl, turning to me.

"You'd better give it to him, don't you know," I said. "He'll go on till you do."

She gave the kid his toffee, and he subsided. Poor old Freddie still stood there gaping, without a word.

"What does it mean?" said the girl again. Her face was pink, and her eyes were sparkling in the sort of way, don't you know, that makes a fellow feel as if he hadn't any bones in him, if you know what I mean. Did you ever tread on your partner's dress at a dance and tear it, and see her smile at you like an angel and say: "*Please* don't apologize. It's nothing," and then suddenly meet her clear blue eyes and feel as if you had stepped on the teeth of a rake and had the handle jump up and hit you in the face? Well, that's how Freddie's Angela looked.

"*Well?*" she said, and her teeth gave a little click.

I gulped. Then I said it was nothing. Then I said it was nothing much. Then I said, "Oh, well, it was this way." And, after a few brief remarks about Jimmy Pinkerton, I told her all about it. And all the while Idiot Freddie stood there gaping, without a word.

And the girl didn't speak, either. She just stood listening.

And then she began to laugh. I never heard a girl laugh so much. She leaned against the side of the veranda and shrieked. And all the while Freddie, the World's Champion Chump, stood there, saying nothing.

Well I sidled towards the steps. I had said all I had to say, and it seemed to me that about here the stage-direction "exit" was written in my part. I gave poor old Freddie up in despair. If only he had said a word, it might have been all right. But there he stood, speechless. What can a fellow do with a fellow like that?

Just out of sight of the house I met Jimmy Pinkerton.

"Hello, Reggie!" he said. "I was just coming to you. Where's the kid? We must have a big rehearsal to-day."

"No good," I said sadly. "It's all over. The thing's finished. Poor dear old Freddie has made an ass of himself and killed the whole show."

"Tell me," said Jimmy.

I told him.

"Fluffed in his lines, did he?" said Jimmy, nodding thoughtfully. "It's always the way with these amateurs. We must go back at once. Things look bad, but it may not be too late," he said as we started. "Even now a few well-chosen words from a man of the world, and——"

"Great Scot!" I cried. "Look!"

In front of the cottage stood six children, a nurse, and the fellow from the grocer's staring. From the windows of the houses opposite projected about four hundred heads of both sexes, staring. Down the road came galloping five more children, a dog, three men, and a boy, about to stare. And on our porch, as unconscious of the spectators as if they had been alone in the Sahara, stood Freddie and Angela, clasped in each other's arms.

Dear old Freddie may have been fluffy in his lines, but, by George, his business had certainly gone with a bang!

CHAPTER - 6

RALLYING ROUND OLD GEORGE

I think one of the rummiest affairs I was ever mixed up with, in the course of a lifetime devoted to butting into other people's business, was that affair of George Lattaker at Monte Carlo. I wouldn't bore you, don't you know, for the world, but I think you ought to hear about it.

We had come to Monte Carlo on the yacht *Circe*, belonging to an old sportsman of the name of Marshall. Among those present were myself, my man Voules, a Mrs. Vanderley, her daughter Stella, Mrs. Vanderley's maid Pilbeam and George.

George was a dear old pal of mine. In fact, it was I who had worked him into the party. You see, George was due to meet his Uncle Augustus, who was scheduled, George having just reached his twenty-fifth birthday, to hand over to him a legacy left by one of George's aunts, for which he had been trustee. The aunt had died when George was quite a kid. It was a date that George had been looking forward to; for, though he had a sort of income—an income, after-all, is only an income, whereas a chunk of o' goblins is a pile. George's uncle was in Monte Carlo, and had written George that he would come to London and unbelt; but it struck me that a far better plan was for George to go to his uncle at Monte Carlo instead. Kill two birds with one stone, don't you know. Fix up his affairs and have a pleasant holiday simultaneously. So George had tagged along, and at the time when the trouble started we were anchored in Monaco Harbour, and Uncle Augustus was due next day.

Looking back, I may say that, so far as I was mixed up in it, the thing began at seven o'clock in the morning, when I was aroused from a dreamless sleep by the dickens of a scrap in progress outside my state-room door. The chief ingredients were a female voice that sobbed and said: "Oh, Harold!" and a male voice "raised in anger," as they say, which after considerable difficulty, I identified as Voules's. I hardly recognized it. In his official capacity Voules talks exactly like you'd expect a statue to talk, if it could. In private, however, he evidently relaxed to some extent, and to have that sort of thing going on in my midst at that hour was too much for me.

"Voules!" I yelled.

Spion Kop ceased with a jerk. There was silence, then sobs diminishing in the distance, and finally a tap at the door. Voules entered with that impressive, my-lord-the-carriage-waits look which is what I pay him for. You wouldn't have believed he had a drop of any sort of emotion in him.

"Voules," I said, "are you under the delusion that I'm going to be Queen of the May? You've called me early all right. It's only just seven."

"I understood you to summon me, sir."

"I summoned you to find out why you were making that infernal noise outside."

"I owe you an apology, sir. I am afraid that in the heat of the moment I raised my voice."

"It's a wonder you didn't raise the roof. Who was that with you?"

"Miss Pilbeam, sir; Mrs. Vanderley's maid."

"What was all the trouble about?"

"I was breaking our engagement, sir."

I couldn't help gaping. Somehow one didn't associate Voules with engagements. Then it struck me that I'd no right to butt in on his secret sorrows, so I switched the conversation.

"I think I'll get up," I said.

"Yes, sir."

"I can't wait to breakfast with the rest. Can you get me some right away?"

"Yes, sir."

So I had a solitary breakfast and went up on deck to smoke. It was a lovely morning. Blue sea, gleaming Casino, cloudless sky, and all the rest of the hippodrome. Presently the others began to trickle up. Stella Vanderley was one of the first. I thought she looked a bit pale and tired. She said she hadn't slept well. That accounted for it. Unless you get your eight hours, where are you?

"Seen George?" I asked.

I couldn't help thinking the name seemed to freeze her a bit. Which was queer, because all the voyage she and George had been particularly close pals. In fact, at any moment I expected George to come to me and slip his little hand in mine, and whisper: "I've done it, old scout; she loves muh!"

"I have not seen Mr. Lattaker," she said.

I didn't pursue the subject. George's stock was apparently low that a.m.

The next item in the day's programme occurred a few minutes later when the morning papers arrived.

Mrs. Vanderley opened hers and gave a scream.

"The poor, dear Prince!" she said.

"What a shocking thing!" said old Marshall.

"I knew him in Vienna," said Mrs. Vanderley. "He waltzed divinely."

Then I got at mine and saw what they were talking about. The paper was full of it. It seemed that late the night before His Serene Highness the Prince of Saxburg-Leignitz (I always wonder why they call these chaps "Serene") had been murderously assaulted in a dark street on his way back from the Casino to his yacht. Apparently he had developed the habit of going about without an escort, and some rough-neck, taking advantage of this, had laid for him and slugged him with considerable vim. The Prince had been found lying pretty well beaten up and insensible in the street by a passing pedestrian, and had been taken back to his yacht, where he still lay unconscious.

"This is going to do somebody no good," I said. "What do you get for slugging a Serene Highness? I wonder if they'll catch the fellow?"

"'Later,'" read old Marshall, "'the pedestrian who discovered His Serene Highness proves to have been Mr. Denman Sturgis, the eminent private investigator. Mr. Sturgis has offered his services to the police, and is understood to be in possession of a most important clue.' That's the fellow who had charge of that kidnapping case in Chicago. If anyone can catch the man, he can."

About five minutes later, just as the rest of them were going to move off to breakfast, a boat hailed us and came alongside. A tall, thin man came up the gangway. He looked round the group, and fixed on old Marshall as the probable owner of the yacht.

"Good morning," he said. "I believe you have a Mr. Lattaker on board—Mr. George Lattaker?"

"Yes," said Marshall. "He's down below. Want to see him? Whom shall I say?"

"He would not know my name. I should like to see him for a moment on somewhat urgent business."

"Take a seat. He'll be up in a moment. Reggie, my boy, go and hurry him up."

I went down to George's state-room.

"George, old man!" I shouted.

No answer. I opened the door and went in. The room was empty. What's more, the bunk hadn't been slept in. I don't know when I've been more surprised. I went on deck.

"He isn't there," I said.

"Not there!" said old Marshall. "Where is he, then? Perhaps he's gone for a stroll ashore. But he'll be back soon for breakfast. You'd better wait for him. Have you breakfasted? No? Then will you join us?"

The man said he would, and just then the gong went and they trooped down, leaving me alone on deck.

I sat smoking and thinking, and then smoking a bit more, when I thought I heard somebody call my name in a sort of hoarse whisper. I looked over my shoulder, and, by Jove, there at the top of the gangway in evening dress, dusty to the eyebrows and without a hat, was dear old George.

"Great Scot!" I cried.

"'Sh!" he whispered. "Anyone about?"

"They're all down at breakfast."

He gave a sigh of relief, sank into my chair, and closed his eyes. I regarded him with pity. The poor old boy looked a wreck.

"I say!" I said, touching him on the shoulder.

He leaped out of the chair with a smothered yell.

"Did you do that? What did you do it for? What's the sense of it? How do you suppose you can ever make yourself popular if you go about touching people on the shoulder? My nerves are sticking a yard out of my body this morning, Reggie!"

"Yes, old boy?"

"I did a murder last night."

"What?"

"It's the sort of thing that might happen to anybody. Directly Stella Vanderley broke off our engagement I——"

"Broke off your engagement? How long were you engaged?"

"About two minutes. It may have been less. I hadn't a stop-watch. I proposed to her at ten last night in the saloon. She accepted me. I was just going to kiss her when we heard someone coming. I went out. Coming along the corridor was that infernal what's-her-name—Mrs. Vanderley's maid—Pilbeam. Have you ever been accepted by the girl you love, Reggie?"

"Never. I've been refused dozens——"

"Then you won't understand how I felt. I was off my head with joy. I hardly knew what I was doing. I just felt I had to kiss the nearest thing handy. I couldn't wait. It might have been the ship's cat. It wasn't. It was Pilbeam."

"You kissed her?"

"I kissed her. And just at that moment the door of the saloon opened and out came Stella."

"Great Scott!"

"Exactly what I said. It flashed across me that to Stella, dear girl, not knowing the circumstances, the thing might seem a little odd. It did. She broke off the engagement, and I got out the dinghy and rowed off. I was mad. I didn't care what became of me. I simply wanted to forget. I went ashore. I—It's just on the cards that I may have drowned my sorrows a bit. Anyhow, I don't remember a thing, except that I can recollect having the deuce of a scrap with somebody in a dark street and somebody falling, and myself falling, and myself legging it for all I was worth. I woke up this morning in the Casino gardens. I've lost my hat."

I dived for the paper.

"Read," I said. "It's all there."

He read.

"Good heavens!" he said.

"You didn't do a thing to His Serene Nibs, did you?"

"Reggie, this is awful."

"Cheer up. They say he'll recover."

"That doesn't matter."

"It does to him."

He read the paper again.

"It says they've a clue."

"They always say that."

"But—My hat!"

"Eh?"

"My hat. I must have dropped it during the scrap. This man, Denman Sturgis, must have found it. It had my name in it!"

"George," I said, "you mustn't waste time. Oh!"

He jumped a foot in the air.

"Don't do it!" he said, irritably. "Don't bark like that. What's the matter?"

"The man!"

"What man?"

"A tall, thin man with an eye like a gimlet. He arrived just before you did. He's down in the saloon now, having breakfast. He said he wanted to see you on business, and wouldn't give his name. I didn't like the look of him from the first. It's this fellow Sturgis. It must be."

"No!"

"I feel it. I'm sure of it."

"Had he a hat?"

"Of course he had a hat."

"Fool! I mean mine. Was he carrying a hat?"

"By Jove, he *was* carrying a parcel. George, old scout, you must get a move on. You must light out if you want to spend the rest of your life out of prison. Slugging a Serene Highness is *lèse-majesté*. It's worse than hitting a policeman. You haven't got a moment to waste."

"But I haven't any money. Reggie, old man, lend me a tenner or something. I must get over the frontier into Italy at once. I'll wire my uncle to meet me in——"

"Look out," I cried; "there's someone coming!"

He dived out of sight just as Voules came up the companion-way, carrying a letter on a tray.

"What's the matter!" I said. "What do you want?"

"I beg your pardon, sir. I thought I heard Mr. Lattaker's voice. A letter has arrived for him."

"He isn't here."

"No, sir. Shall I remove the letter?"

"No; give it to me. I'll give it to him when he comes."

"Very good, sir."

"Oh, Voules! Are they all still at breakfast? The gentleman who came to see Mr. Lattaker? Still hard at it?"

"He is at present occupied with a kippered herring, sir."

"Ah! That's all, Voules."

"Thank you, sir."

He retired. I called to George, and he came out.

"Who was it?"

"Only Voules. He brought a letter for you. They're all at breakfast still. The sleuth's eating kippers."

"That'll hold him for a bit. Full of bones." He began to read his letter. He gave a kind of grunt of surprise at the first paragraph.

"Well, I'm hanged!" he said, as he finished.

"Reggie, this is a queer thing."

"What's that?"

He handed me the letter, and directly I started in on it I saw why he had grunted. This is how it ran:

"My dear George—I shall be seeing you to-morrow, I hope; but I think it is better, before we meet, to prepare you for a curious situation that has arisen in connection with the legacy which your father inherited from your Aunt Emily, and which you are expecting me, as trustee, to hand over to you, now that you have reached your twenty-fifth birthday. You have doubtless heard your father speak of your twin-brother Alfred, who was lost or kidnapped—which, was never ascertained—when you were both babies. When no news was received of him for so many years, it was supposed that he was dead. Yesterday, however, I received a letter purporting that he had been living all this time in Buenos Ayres as the adopted son of a wealthy South American, and has only recently discovered his identity. He states that he is on his way to meet me, and will arrive any day now. Of course, like other claimants, he may prove to be an impostor, but meanwhile his intervention will, I fear, cause a certain delay before I can hand over your money to you. It will be necessary to go into a thorough examination of credentials, etc., and this will take some time. But I will go fully into the matter with you when we meet.—Your affectionate uncle,

"AUGUSTUS ARBUTT."

I read it through twice, and the second time I had one of those ideas I do sometimes get, though admittedly a chump of the premier class. I have seldom had such a thoroughly corking brain-wave.

"Why, old top," I said, "this lets you out."

"Lets me out of half the darned money, if that's what you mean. If this chap's not an imposter—and there's no earthly reason to suppose he is, though

I've never heard my father say a word about him—we shall have to split the money. Aunt Emily's will left the money to my father, or, failing him, his 'offspring.' I thought that meant me, but apparently there are a crowd of us. I call it rotten work, springing unexpected offspring on a fellow at the eleventh hour like this."

"Why, you chump," I said, "it's going to save you. This lets you out of your spectacular dash across the frontier. All you've got to do is to stay here and be your brother Alfred. It came to me in a flash."

He looked at me in a kind of dazed way.

"You ought to be in some sort of a home, Reggie."

"Ass!" I cried. "Don't you understand? Have you ever heard of twin-brothers who weren't exactly alike? Who's to say you aren't Alfred if you swear you are? Your uncle will be there to back you up that you have a brother Alfred."

"And Alfred will be there to call me a liar."

"He won't. It's not as if you had to keep it up for the rest of your life. It's only for an hour or two, till we can get this detective off the yacht. We sail for England to-morrow morning."

At last the thing seemed to sink into him. His face brightened.

"Why, I really do believe it would work," he said.

"Of course it would work. If they want proof, show them your mole. I'll swear George hadn't one."

"And as Alfred I should get a chance of talking to Stella and making things all right for George. Reggie, old top, you're a genius."

"No, no."

"You *are*."

"Well, it's only sometimes. I can't keep it up."

And just then there was a gentle cough behind us. We spun round.

"What the devil are you doing here, Voules," I said.

"I beg your pardon, sir. I have heard all."

I looked at George. George looked at me.

"Voules is all right," I said. "Decent Voules! Voules wouldn't give us away, would you, Voules?"

"Yes, sir."

"You would?"

"Yes, sir."

"But, Voules, old man," I said, "be sensible. What would you gain by it?"

"Financially, sir, nothing."

"Whereas, by keeping quiet"—I tapped him on the chest—"by holding your tongue, Voules, by saying nothing about it to anybody, Voules, old fellow, you might gain a considerable sum."

"Am I to understand, sir, that, because you are rich and I am poor, you think that you can buy my self-respect?"

"Oh, come!" I said.

"How much?" said Voules.

So we switched to terms. You wouldn't believe the way the man haggled. You'd have thought a decent, faithful servant would have been delighted to oblige one in a little matter like that for a fiver. But not Voules. By no means. It was a hundred down, and the promise of another hundred when we had got safely away, before he was satisfied. But we fixed it up at last, and poor old George got down to his state-room and changed his clothes.

He'd hardly gone when the breakfast-party came on deck.

"Did you meet him?" I asked.

"Meet whom?" said old Marshall.

"George's twin-brother Alfred."

"I didn't know George had a brother."

"Nor did he till yesterday. It's a long story. He was kidnapped in infancy, and everyone thought he was dead. George had a letter from his uncle about him yesterday. I shouldn't wonder if that's where George has gone, to see his uncle and find out about it. In the meantime, Alfred has arrived. He's down in George's state-room now, having a brush-up. It'll amaze you, the likeness between them. You'll think it *is* George at first. Look! Here he comes."

And up came George, brushed and clean, in an ordinary yachting suit.

They were rattled. There was no doubt about that. They stood looking at him, as if they thought there was a catch somewhere, but weren't quite certain where it was. I introduced him, and still they looked doubtful.

"Mr. Pepper tells me my brother is not on board," said George.

"It's an amazing likeness," said old Marshall.

"Is my brother like me?" asked George amiably.

"No one could tell you apart," I said.

"I suppose twins always are alike," said George. "But if it ever came to a question of identification, there would be one way of distinguishing us. Do you know George well, Mr. Pepper?"

"He's a dear old pal of mine."

"You've been swimming with him perhaps?"

"Every day last August."

"Well, then, you would have noticed it if he had had a mole like this on the back of his neck, wouldn't you?" He turned his back and stooped and showed the mole. His collar hid it at ordinary times. I had seen it often when we were bathing together.

"Has George a mole like that?" he asked.

"No," I said. "Oh, no."

"You would have noticed it if he had?"

"Yes," I said. "Oh, yes."

"I'm glad of that," said George. "It would be a nuisance not to be able to prove one's own identity."

That seemed to satisfy them all. They couldn't get away from it. It seemed to me that from now on the thing was a walk-over. And I think George felt the same, for, when old Marshall asked him if he had had breakfast, he said he had not, went below, and pitched in as if he hadn't a care in the world.

Everything went right till lunch-time. George sat in the shade on the foredeck talking to Stella most of the time. When the gong went and the rest had started to go below, he drew me back. He was beaming.

"It's all right," he said. "What did I tell you?"

"What did you tell me?"

"Why, about Stella. Didn't I say that Alfred would fix things for George? I told her she looked worried, and got her to tell me what the trouble was. And then——"

"You must have shown a flash of speed if you got her to confide in you after knowing you for about two hours."

"Perhaps I did," said George modestly, "I had no notion, till I became him, what a persuasive sort of chap my brother Alfred was. Anyway, she told me all about it, and I started in to show her that George was a pretty good sort of fellow on the whole, who oughtn't to be turned down for what was evidently merely temporary insanity. She saw my point."

"And it's all right?"

"Absolutely, if only we can produce George. How much longer does that infernal sleuth intend to stay here? He seems to have taken root."

"I fancy he thinks that you're bound to come back sooner or later, and is waiting for you."

"He's an absolute nuisance," said George.

We were moving towards the companion way, to go below for lunch, when a boat hailed us. We went to the side and looked over.

"It's my uncle," said George.

A stout man came up the gangway.

"Halloa, George!" he said. "Get my letter?"

"I think you are mistaking me for my brother," said George. "My name is Alfred Lattaker."

"What's that?"

"I am George's brother Alfred. Are you my Uncle Augustus?"

The stout man stared at him.

"You're very like George," he said.

"So everyone tells me."

"And you're really Alfred?"

"I am."

"I'd like to talk business with you for a moment."

He cocked his eye at me. I sidled off and went below.

At the foot of the companion-steps I met Voules.

"I beg your pardon, sir," said Voules. "If it would be convenient I should be glad to have the afternoon off."

I'm bound to say I rather liked his manner. Absolutely normal. Not a trace of the fellow-conspirator about it. I gave him the afternoon off.

I had lunch—George didn't show up—and as I was going out I was waylaid by the girl Pilbeam. She had been crying.

"I beg your pardon, sir, but did Mr. Voules ask you for the afternoon?"

I didn't see what business if was of hers, but she seemed all worked up about it, so I told her.

"Yes, I have given him the afternoon off."

She broke down—absolutely collapsed. Devilish unpleasant it was. I'm hopeless in a situation like this. After I'd said, "There, there!" which didn't seem to help much, I hadn't any remarks to make.

"He s-said he was going to the tables to gamble away all his savings and then shoot himself, because he had nothing left to live for."

I suddenly remembered the scrap in the small hours outside my state-room door. I hate mysteries. I meant to get to the bottom of this. I couldn't have a really first-class valet like Voules going about the place shooting himself up. Evidently the girl Pilbeam was at the bottom of the thing. I questioned her. She sobbed.

I questioned her more. I was firm. And eventually she yielded up the facts. Voules had seen George kiss her the night before; that was the trouble.

Things began to piece themselves together. I went up to interview George. There was going to be another job for persuasive Alfred. Voules's mind had got to be eased as Stella's had been. I couldn't afford to lose a fellow with his genius for preserving a trouser-crease.

I found George on the foredeck. What is it Shakespeare or somebody says about some fellow's face being sicklied o'er with the pale cast of care? George's was like that. He looked green.

"Finished with your uncle?" I said.

He grinned a ghostly grin.

"There isn't any uncle," he said. "There isn't any Alfred. And there isn't any money."

"Explain yourself, old top," I said.

"It won't take long. The old crook has spent every penny of the trust money. He's been at it for years, ever since I was a kid. When the time came to cough up, and I was due to see that he did it, he went to the tables in the hope of a run of luck, and lost the last remnant of the stuff. He had to find a way of holding me for a while and postponing the squaring of accounts while he got away, and he invented this twin-brother business. He knew I should find out sooner or later, but meanwhile he would be able to get off to South America, which he has done. He's on his way now."

"You let him go?"

"What could I do? I can't afford to make a fuss with that man Sturgis around. I can't prove there's no Alfred when my only chance of avoiding prison is to be Alfred."

"Well, you've made things right for yourself with Stella Vanderley, anyway," I said, to cheer him up.

"What's the good of that now? I've hardly any money and no prospects. How can I marry her?"

I pondered.

"It looks to me, old top," I said at last, "as if things were in a bit of a mess."

"You've guessed it," said poor old George.

I spent the afternoon musing on Life. If you come to think of it, what a queer thing Life is! So unlike anything else, don't you know, if you see what I mean. At any moment you may be strolling peacefully along, and all the time Life's waiting around the corner to fetch you one. You can't tell when you may be going to get it. It's all dashed puzzling. Here was poor old George, as well-meaning a fellow as ever stepped, getting swatted all over the ring by the hand of Fate. Why? That's what I asked myself. Just Life, don't you know. That's all there was about it.

It was close on six o'clock when our third visitor of the day arrived. We were sitting on the afterdeck in the cool of the evening—old Marshall, Denman Sturgis, Mrs. Vanderley, Stella, George, and I—when he came up. We had been talking of George, and old Marshall was suggesting the advisability of sending out search-parties. He was worried. So was Stella Vanderley. So, for that matter, were George and I, only not for the same reason.

We were just arguing the thing out when the visitor appeared. He was a well-built, stiff sort of fellow. He spoke with a German accent.

"Mr. Marshall?" he said. "I am Count Fritz von Cöslin, equerry to His Serene Highness"—he clicked his heels together and saluted—"the Prince of Saxburg-Leignitz."

Mrs. Vanderley jumped up.

"Why, Count," she said, "what ages since we met in Vienna! You remember?"

"Could I ever forget? And the charming Miss Stella, she is well, I suppose not?"

"Stella, you remember Count Fritz?"

Stella shook hands with him.

"And how is the poor, dear Prince?" asked Mrs. Vanderley. "What a terrible thing to have happened!"

"I rejoice to say that my high-born master is better. He has regained consciousness and is sitting up and taking nourishment."

"That's good," said old Marshall.

"In a spoon only," sighed the Count. "Mr. Marshall, with your permission I should like a word with Mr. Sturgis."

"Mr. Who?"

The gimlet-eyed sportsman came forward.

"I am Denman Sturgis, at your service."

"The deuce you are! What are you doing here?"

"Mr. Sturgis," explained the Count, "graciously volunteered his services"

"I know. But what's he doing here?"

"I am waiting for Mr. George Lattaker, Mr. Marshall."

"Eh?"

"You have not found him?" asked the Count anxiously.

"Not yet, Count; but I hope to do so shortly. I know what he looks like now. This gentleman is his twin-brother. They are doubles."

"You are sure this gentleman is not Mr. George Lattaker?"

George put his foot down firmly on the suggestion.

"Don't go mixing me up with my brother," he said. "I am Alfred. You can tell me by my mole."

He exhibited the mole. He was taking no risks.

The Count clicked his tongue regretfully.

"I am sorry," he said.

George didn't offer to console him,

"Don't worry," said Sturgis. "He won't escape me. I shall find him."

"Do, Mr. Sturgis, do. And quickly. Find swiftly that noble young man."

"What?" shouted George.

"That noble young man, George Lattaker, who, at the risk of his life, saved my high-born master from the assassin."

George sat down suddenly.

"I don't understand," he said feebly.

"We were wrong, Mr. Sturgis," went on the Count. "We leaped to the conclusion—was it not so?—that the owner of the hat you found was also the assailant of my high-born master. We were wrong. I have heard the story from His Serene Highness's own lips. He was passing down a dark street when a ruffian in a mask sprang out upon him. Doubtless he had been followed from the Casino, where he had been winning heavily. My high-born master was taken by surprise. He was felled. But before he lost consciousness he perceived a young man in evening dress, wearing the hat you found, running swiftly towards him. The hero engaged the assassin in combat, and my high-born master remembers no more. His Serene Highness asks repeatedly, 'Where is my brave preserver?' His gratitude is princely. He seeks for this young man to reward him. Ah, you should be proud of your brother, sir!"

"Thanks," said George limply.

"And you, Mr. Sturgis, you must redouble your efforts. You must search the land; you must scour the sea to find George Lattaker."

"He needn't take all that trouble," said a voice from the gangway.

It was Voules. His face was flushed, his hat was on the back of his head, and he was smoking a fat cigar.

"I'll tell you where to find George Lattaker!" he shouted.

He glared at George, who was staring at him.

"Yes, look at me," he yelled. "Look at me. You won't be the first this afternoon who's stared at the mysterious stranger who won for two hours without a break. I'll be even with you now, Mr. Blooming Lattaker. I'll learn you to break a poor man's heart. Mr. Marshall and gents, this morning I was on deck, and I over'eard 'im plotting to put up a game on you. They'd spotted that gent there as a detective, and they arranged that blooming Lattaker was to pass himself off as his own twin-brother. And if you wanted proof, blooming Pepper tells him to show them his mole and he'd swear George hadn't one. Those were his very words. That man there is George Lattaker, Hesquire, and let him deny it if he can."

George got up.

"I haven't the least desire to deny it, Voules."

"Mr. Voules, if *you* please."

"It's true," said George, turning to the Count. "The fact is, I had rather a foggy recollection of what happened last night. I only remembered knocking some one down, and, like you, I jumped to the conclusion that I must have assaulted His Serene Highness."

"Then you are really George Lattaker?" asked the Count.

"I am."

"'Ere, what does all this mean?" demanded Voules.

"Merely that I saved the life of His Serene Highness the Prince of Saxburg-Leignitz, Mr. Voules."

"It's a swindle!" began Voules, when there was a sudden rush and the girl Pilbeam cannoned into the crowd, sending me into old Marshall's chair, and flung herself into the arms of Voules.

"Oh, Harold!" she cried. "I thought you were dead. I thought you'd shot yourself."

He sort of braced himself together to fling her off, and then he seemed to think better of it and fell into the clinch.

It was all dashed romantic, don't you know, but there *are* limits.

"Voules, you're sacked," I said.

"Who cares?" he said. "Think I was going to stop on now I'm a gentleman of property? Come along, Emma, my dear. Give a month's notice and get your 'at, and I'll take you to dinner at Ciro's."

"And you, Mr. Lattaker," said the Count, "may I conduct you to the presence of my high-born master? He wishes to show his gratitude to his preserver."

"You may," said George. "May I have my hat, Mr. Sturgis?"

There's just one bit more. After dinner that night I came up for a smoke, and, strolling on to the foredeck, almost bumped into George and Stella. They seemed to be having an argument.

"I'm not sure," she was saying, "that I believe that a man can be so happy that he wants to kiss the nearest thing in sight, as you put it."

"Don't you?" said George. "Well, as it happens, I'm feeling just that way now."

I coughed and he turned round.

"Halloa, Reggie!" he said.

"Halloa, George!" I said. "Lovely night."

"Beautiful," said Stella.

"The moon," I said.

"Ripping," said George.

"Lovely," said Stella.

"And look at the reflection of the stars on the——"

George caught my eye. "Pop off," he said.

I popped.

Chapter - 7

DOING CLARENCE A BIT OF GOOD

Have you ever thought about—and, when I say thought about, I mean really carefully considered the question of—the coolness, the cheek, or, if you prefer it, the gall with which Woman, as a sex, fairly bursts? *I* have, by Jove! But then I've had it thrust on my notice, by George, in a way I should imagine has happened to pretty few fellows. And the limit was reached by that business of the Yeardsley "Venus."

To make you understand the full what-d'you-call-it of the situation, I shall have to explain just how matters stood between Mrs. Yeardsley and myself.

When I first knew her she was Elizabeth Shoolbred. Old Worcestershire family; pots of money; pretty as a picture. Her brother Bill was at Oxford with me.

I loved Elizabeth Shoolbred. I loved her, don't you know. And there was a time, for about a week, when we were engaged to be married. But just as I was beginning to take a serious view of life and study furniture catalogues and feel pretty solemn when the restaurant orchestra played "The Wedding Glide," I'm hanged if she didn't break it off, and a month later she was married to a fellow of the name of Yeardsley—Clarence Yeardsley, an artist.

What with golf, and billiards, and a bit of racing, and fellows at the club rallying round and kind of taking me out of myself, as it were, I got over it, and came to look on the affair as a closed page in the book of my life, if you know what I mean. It didn't seem likely to me that we should meet again, as she and Clarence had settled down in the country somewhere and never came to London, and I'm bound to own that, by the time I got her letter, the wound had pretty well healed, and I was to a certain extent sitting up and taking nourishment. In fact, to be absolutely honest, I was jolly thankful the thing had ended as it had done.

This letter I'm telling you about arrived one morning out of a blue sky, as it were. It ran like this:

"MY DEAR OLD REGGIE,—What ages it seems since I saw anything of you. How are you? We have settled down here in the most perfect old house, with a lovely garden, in the middle of delightful country. Couldn't you run down here for a few days? Clarence and I would be so glad to see you. Bill is here, and is most anxious to meet you again. He was speaking of you only this morning. *Do* come. Wire your train, and I will send the car to meet you.

—Yours most sincerely,

ELIZABETH YEARDSLEY.

"P.S.—We can give you new milk and fresh eggs. Think of that!

"P.P.S.—Bill says our billiard-table is one of the best he has ever played on.

"P.P.S.S.—We are only half a mile from a golf course. Bill says it is better than St. Andrews.

"P.P.S.S.S.—You *must* come!"

Well, a fellow comes down to breakfast one morning, with a bit of a head on, and finds a letter like that from a girl who might quite easily have blighted his life! It rattled me rather, I must confess.

However, that bit about the golf settled me. I knew Bill knew what he was talking about, and, if he said the course was so topping, it must be something special. So I went.

Old Bill met me at the station with the car. I hadn't come across him for some months, and I was glad to see him again. And he apparently was glad to see me.

"Thank goodness you've come," he said, as we drove off. "I was just about at my last grip."

"What's the trouble, old scout?" I asked.

"If I had the artistic what's-its-name," he went on, "if the mere mention of pictures didn't give me the pip, I dare say it wouldn't be so bad. As it is, it's rotten!"

"Pictures?"

"Pictures. Nothing else is mentioned in this household. Clarence is an artist. So is his father. And you know yourself what Elizabeth is like when one gives her her head?"

I remembered then—it hadn't come back to me before—that most of my time with Elizabeth had been spent in picture-galleries. During the period when I had let her do just what she wanted to do with me, I had had to follow her like a dog through gallery after gallery, though pictures are poison to me, just as they are to old Bill. Somehow it had never struck me that she would still be going on in this way after marrying an artist. I should have thought that by this time the mere sight of a picture would have fed her up. Not so, however, according to old Bill.

"They talk pictures at every meal," he said. "I tell you, it makes a chap feel out of it. How long are you down for?"

"A few days."

"Take my tip, and let me send you a wire from London. I go there to-morrow. I promised to play against the Scottish. The idea was that I was to come back after the match. But you couldn't get me back with a lasso."

I tried to point out the silver lining.

"But, Bill, old scout, your sister says there's a most corking links near here."

He turned and stared at me, and nearly ran us into the bank.

"You don't mean honestly she said that?"

"She said you said it was better than St. Andrews."

"So I did. Was that all she said I said?"

"Well, wasn't it enough?"

"She didn't happen to mention that I added the words, 'I don't think'?"

"No, she forgot to tell me that."

"It's the worst course in Great Britain."

I felt rather stunned, don't you know. Whether it's a bad habit to have got into or not, I can't say, but I simply can't do without my daily allowance of golf when I'm not in London.

I took another whirl at the silver lining.

"We'll have to take it out in billiards," I said. "I'm glad the table's good."

"It depends what you call good. It's half-size, and there's a seven-inch cut just out of baulk where Clarence's cue slipped. Elizabeth has mended it with pink silk. Very smart and dressy it looks, but it doesn't improve the thing as a billiard-table."

"But she said you said——"

"Must have been pulling your leg."

We turned in at the drive gates of a good-sized house standing well back from the road. It looked black and sinister in the dusk, and I couldn't help feeling, you know, like one of those Johnnies you read about in stories who are lured to lonely houses for rummy purposes and hear a shriek just as they get there. Elizabeth knew me well enough to know that a specially good golf course was a safe draw to me. And she had deliberately played on her knowledge. What was the game? That was what I wanted to know. And then a sudden thought struck me which brought me out in a cold perspiration. She had some girl down here and was going to have a stab at marrying me off. I've often heard that young married women are all over that sort of thing. Certainly she had said there was nobody at the house but Clarence and herself and Bill and Clarence's father, but a woman who could take the name of St. Andrews in vain as she had done wouldn't be likely to stick at a trifle.

"Bill, old scout," I said, "there aren't any frightful girls or any rot of that sort stopping here, are there?"

"Wish there were," he said. "No such luck."

As we pulled up at the front door, it opened, and a woman's figure appeared.

"Have you got him, Bill?" she said, which in my present frame of mind struck me as a jolly creepy way of putting it. The sort of thing Lady Macbeth might have said to Macbeth, don't you know.

"Do you mean me?" I said.

She came down into the light. It was Elizabeth, looking just the same as in the old days.

"Is that you, Reggie? I'm so glad you were able to come. I was afraid you might have forgotten all about it. You know what you are. Come along in and have some tea."

Have you ever been turned down by a girl who afterwards married and then been introduced to her husband? If so you'll understand how I felt when Clarence burst on me. You know the feeling. First of all, when you hear about the marriage, you say to yourself, "I wonder what he's like." Then you meet him, and think, "There must be some mistake. She can't have preferred *this* to me!" That's what I thought, when I set eyes on Clarence.

He was a little thin, nervous-looking chappie of about thirty-five. His hair was getting grey at the temples and straggly on top. He wore pince-nez, and he had a drooping moustache. I'm no Bombardier Wells myself, but in front of Clarence I felt quite a nut. And Elizabeth, mind you, is one of those tall, splendid girls who look like princesses. Honestly, I believe women do it out of pure cussedness.

"How do you do, Mr. Pepper? Hark! Can you hear a mewing cat?" said Clarence. All in one breath, don't you know.

"Eh?" I said.

"A mewing cat. I feel sure I hear a mewing cat. Listen!"

While we were listening the door opened, and a white-haired old gentleman came in. He was built on the same lines as Clarence, but was an earlier model. I took him correctly, to be Mr. Yeardsley, senior. Elizabeth introduced us.

"Father," said Clarence, "did you meet a mewing cat outside? I feel positive I heard a cat mewing."

"No," said the father, shaking his head; "no mewing cat."

"I can't bear mewing cats," said Clarence. "A mewing cat gets on my nerves!"

"A mewing cat is so trying," said Elizabeth.

"*I* dislike mewing cats," said old Mr. Yeardsley.

That was all about mewing cats for the moment. They seemed to think they had covered the ground satisfactorily, and they went back to pictures.

We talked pictures steadily till it was time to dress for dinner. At least, they did. I just sort of sat around. Presently the subject of picture-robberies came up. Somebody mentioned the "Monna Lisa," and then I happened to remember seeing something in the evening paper, as I was coming down in the train, about some fellow somewhere having had a valuable painting pinched by burglars the night before. It was the first time I had had a chance of breaking into the conversation with any effect, and I meant to make the most of it. The paper was in the pocket of my overcoat in the hall. I went and fetched it.

"Here it is," I said. "A Romney belonging to Sir Bellamy Palmer——"

They all shouted "What!" exactly at the same time, like a chorus. Elizabeth grabbed the paper.

"Let me look! Yes. 'Late last night burglars entered the residence of Sir Bellamy Palmer, Dryden Park, Midford, Hants——'"

"Why, that's near here," I said. "I passed through Midford——"

"Dryden Park is only two miles from this house," said Elizabeth. I noticed her eyes were sparkling.

"Only two miles!" she said. "It might have been us! It might have been the 'Venus'!"

Old Mr. Yeardsley bounded in his chair.

"The 'Venus'!" he cried.

They all seemed wonderfully excited. My little contribution to the evening's chat had made quite a hit.

Why I didn't notice it before I don't know, but it was not till Elizabeth showed it to me after dinner that I had my first look at the Yeardsley "Venus." When she led me up to it, and switched on the light, it seemed impossible that I could have sat right through dinner without noticing it. But then, at meals, my attention is pretty well riveted on the foodstuffs. Anyway, it was not till Elizabeth showed it to me that I was aware of its existence.

She and I were alone in the drawing-room after dinner. Old Yeardsley was writing letters in the morning-room, while Bill and Clarence were rollicking on the half-size billiard table with the pink silk tapestry effects. All, in fact, was joy, jollity, and song, so to speak, when Elizabeth, who had been sitting wrapped in thought for a bit, bent towards me and said, "Reggie."

And the moment she said it I knew something was going to happen. You know that pre-what-d'you-call-it you get sometimes? Well, I got it then.

"What-o?" I said nervously.

"Reggie," she said, "I want to ask a great favour of you."

"Yes?"

She stooped down and put a log on the fire, and went on, with her back to me:

"Do you remember, Reggie, once saying you would do anything in the world for me?"

There! That's what I meant when I said that about the cheek of Woman as a sex. What I mean is, after what had happened, you'd have thought she would have preferred to let the dead past bury its dead, and all that sort of thing, what?

Mind you, I *had* said I would do anything in the world for her. I admit that. But it was a distinctly pre-Clarence remark. He hadn't appeared on the scene then, and it stands to reason that a fellow who may have been a perfect knight-errant to a girl when he was engaged to her, doesn't feel nearly so keen on spreading himself in that direction when she has given him the miss-in-baulk, and gone and married a man who reason and instinct both tell him is a decided blighter.

I couldn't think of anything to say but "Oh, yes."

"There's something you can do for me now, which will make me everlastingly grateful."

"Yes," I said.

"Do you know, Reggie," she said suddenly, "that only a few months ago Clarence was very fond of cats?"

"Eh! Well, he still seems—er—*interested* in them, what?"

"Now they get on his nerves. Everything gets on his nerves."

"Some fellows swear by that stuff you see advertised all over the——"

"No, that wouldn't help him. He doesn't need to take anything. He wants to get rid of something."

"I don't quite fellow. Get rid of something?"

"The 'Venus,'" said Elizabeth.

She looked up and caught my bulging eye.

"You saw the 'Venus,'" she said.

"Not that I remember."

"Well, come into the dining-room."

We went into the dining-room, and she switched on the lights.

"There," she said.

On the wall close to the door—that may have been why I hadn't noticed it before; I had sat with my back to it—was a large oil-painting. It was what you'd call a classical picture, I suppose. What I mean is—well, you know what I mean. All I can say is that it's funny I *hadn't* noticed it.

"Is that the 'Venus'?" I said.

She nodded.

"How would you like to have to look at that every time you sat down to a meal?"

"Well, I don't know. I don't think it would affect me much. I'd worry through all right."

She jerked her head impatiently.

"But you're not an artist," she said. "Clarence is."

And then I began to see daylight. What exactly was the trouble I didn't understand, but it was evidently something to do with the good old Artistic Temperament, and I could believe anything about that. It explains everything. It's like the Unwritten Law, don't you know, which you plead in America if you've done anything they want to send you to chokey for and you don't want to go. What I mean is, if you're absolutely off your rocker, but don't find it convenient to be scooped into the luny-bin, you simply explain that, when you said you were a teapot, it was just your Artistic Temperament, and they apologize and go away. So I stood by to hear just how the A.T. had affected Clarence, the Cat's Friend, ready for anything.

And, believe me, it had hit Clarence badly.

It was this way. It seemed that old Yeardsley was an amateur artist and that this "Venus" was his masterpiece. He said so, and he ought to have known. Well, when Clarence married, he had given it to him, as a wedding present, and had hung it where it stood with his own hands. All right so far, what? But mark the sequel. Temperamental Clarence, being a professional artist and consequently some streets ahead of the dad at the game, saw flaws in the "Venus." He couldn't stand it at any price. He didn't like the drawing. He didn't like the expression of the face. He didn't like the colouring. In fact, it made him feel quite ill to look at it. Yet, being devoted to his father and wanting to do anything rather than give him pain, he had not been able to bring himself to store the thing in the cellar, and the strain of confronting the picture three times a day had begun to tell on him to such an extent that Elizabeth felt something had to be done.

"Now you see," she said.

"In a way," I said. "But don't you think it's making rather heavy weather over a trifle?"

"Oh, can't you understand? Look!" Her voice dropped as if she was in church, and she switched on another light. It shone on the picture next to old Yeardsley's. "There!" she said. "Clarence painted that!"

She looked at me expectantly, as if she were waiting for me to swoon, or yell, or something. I took a steady look at Clarence's effort. It was another Classical picture. It seemed to me very much like the other one.

Some sort of art criticism was evidently expected of me, so I made a dash at it.

"Er—'Venus'?" I said.

Mark you, Sherlock Holmes would have made the same mistake. On the evidence, I mean.

"No. 'Jocund Spring,'" she snapped. She switched off the light. "I see you don't understand even now. You never had any taste about pictures. When we used to go to the galleries together, you would far rather have been at your club."

This was so absolutely true, that I had no remark to make. She came up to me, and put her hand on my arm.

"I'm sorry, Reggie. I didn't mean to be cross. Only I do want to make you understand that Clarence is *suffering*. Suppose—suppose—well, let us take the case of a great musician. Suppose a great musician had to sit and listen to a cheap vulgar tune—the same tune—day after day, day after day, wouldn't you expect his nerves to break! Well, it's just like that with Clarence. Now you see?"

"Yes, but——"

"But what? Surely I've put it plainly enough?"

"Yes. But what I mean is, where do I come in? What do you want me to do?"

"I want you to steal the 'Venus.'"

I looked at her.

"You want me to——?"

"Steal it. Reggie!" Her eyes were shining with excitement. "Don't you see? It's Providence. When I asked you to come here, I had just got the idea. I knew I could rely on you. And then by a miracle this robbery of the Romney takes place at a house not two miles away. It removes the last chance of the poor old man suspecting anything and having his feelings hurt. Why, it's the most wonderful compliment to him. Think! One night thieves steal a splendid Romney; the next the same gang take his 'Venus.' It will be the proudest moment of his life. Do it to-night, Reggie. I'll give you a sharp knife. You simply cut the canvas out of the frame, and it's done."

"But one moment," I said. "I'd be delighted to be of any use to you, but in a purely family affair like this, wouldn't it be better—in fact, how about tackling old Bill on the subject?"

"I have asked Bill already. Yesterday. He refused."

"But if I'm caught?"

"You can't be. All you have to do is to take the picture, open one of the windows, leave it open, and go back to your room."

It sounded simple enough.

"And as to the picture itself—when I've got it?"

"Burn it. I'll see that you have a good fire in your room."

"But——"

She looked at me. She always did have the most wonderful eyes.

"Reggie," she said; nothing more. Just "Reggie."

She looked at me.

"Well, after all, if you see what I mean—The days that are no more, don't you know. Auld Lang Syne, and all that sort of thing. You follow me?"

"All right," I said. "I'll do it."

I don't know if you happen to be one of those Johnnies who are steeped in crime, and so forth, and think nothing of pinching diamond necklaces. If you're not, you'll understand that I felt a lot less keen on the job I'd taken on when I sat in my room, waiting to get busy, than I had done when I promised to tackle it in the dining-room. On paper it all seemed easy enough, but I couldn't help feeling there was a catch somewhere, and I've never known time pass slower. The kick-off was scheduled for one o'clock in the morning, when the household might be expected to be pretty sound asleep, but at a quarter to I couldn't stand it any longer. I lit the lantern I had taken from Bill's bicycle, took a grip of my knife, and slunk downstairs.

The first thing I did on getting to the dining-room was to open the window. I had half a mind to smash it, so as to give an extra bit of local colour to the affair, but decided not to on account of the noise. I had put my lantern on the table, and was just reaching out for it, when something happened. What it was for the moment I couldn't have said. It might have been an explosion of some sort or an earthquake. Some solid object caught me a frightful whack on the chin. Sparks and things occurred inside my head and the next thing I remember is feeling something wet and cold splash into my face, and hearing a voice that sounded like old Bill's say, "Feeling better now?"

I sat up. The lights were on, and I was on the floor, with old Bill kneeling beside me with a soda siphon.

"What happened?" I said.

"I'm awfully sorry, old man," he said. "I hadn't a notion it was you. I came in here, and saw a lantern on the table, and the window open and a chap with a knife in his hand, so I didn't stop to make inquiries. I just let go at his jaw for all I was worth. What on earth do you think you're doing? Were you walking in your sleep?"

"It was Elizabeth," I said. "Why, you know all about it. She said she had told you."

"You don't mean——"

"The picture. You refused to take it on, so she asked me."

"Reggie, old man," he said. "I'll never believe what they say about repentance again. It's a fool's trick and upsets everything. If I hadn't repented, and thought it was rather rough on Elizabeth not to do a little thing like that for her, and come down here to do it after all, you wouldn't have stopped that sleep-producer with your chin. I'm sorry."

"Me, too," I said, giving my head another shake to make certain it was still on.

"Are you feeling better now?"

"Better than I was. But that's not saying much."

"Would you like some more soda-water? No? Well, how about getting this job finished and going to bed? And let's be quick about it too. You made a noise like a ton of bricks when you went down just now, and it's on the cards some of the servants may have heard. Toss you who carves."

"Heads."

"Tails it is," he said, uncovering the coin. "Up you get. I'll hold the light. Don't spike yourself on that sword of yours."

It was as easy a job as Elizabeth had said. Just four quick cuts, and the thing came out of its frame like an oyster. I rolled it up. Old Bill had put the lantern on the floor and was at the sideboard, collecting whisky, soda, and glasses.

"We've got a long evening before us," he said. "You can't burn a picture of that size in one chunk. You'd set the chimney on fire. Let's do the thing comfortably. Clarence can't grudge us the stuff. We've done him a bit of good this trip. To-morrow'll be the maddest, merriest day of Clarence's glad New Year. On we go."

We went up to my room, and sat smoking and yarning away and sipping our drinks, and every now and then cutting a slice off the picture and shoving it in the fire till it was all gone. And what with the cosiness of it and the cheerful blaze, and the comfortable feeling of doing good by stealth, I don't know when I've had a jollier time since the days when we used to brew in my study at school.

We had just put the last slice on when Bill sat up suddenly, and gripped my arm.

"I heard something," he said.

I listened, and, by Jove, I heard something, too. My room was just over the dining-room, and the sound came up to us quite distinctly. Stealthy footsteps, by George! And then a chair falling over.

"There's somebody in the dining-room," I whispered.

There's a certain type of chap who takes a pleasure in positively chivvying trouble. Old Bill's like that. If I had been alone, it would have taken me about three seconds to persuade myself that I hadn't really heard anything after all. I'm a peaceful sort of cove, and believe in living and letting live, and so forth. To old Bill, however, a visit from burglars was pure jam. He was out of his chair in one jump.

"Come on," he said. "Bring the poker."

I brought the tongs as well. I felt like it. Old Bill collared the knife. We crept downstairs.

"We'll fling the door open and make a rush," said Bill.

"Supposing they shoot, old scout?"

"Burglars never shoot," said Bill.

Which was comforting provided the burglars knew it.

Old Bill took a grip of the handle, turned it quickly, and in he went.

And then we pulled up sharp, staring.

The room was in darkness except for a feeble splash of light at the near end. Standing on a chair in front of Clarence's "Jocund Spring," holding a candle in one hand and reaching up with a knife in the other, was old Mr. Yeardsley, in bedroom slippers and a grey dressing-gown. He had made a final cut just as we rushed in. Turning at the sound, he stopped, and he and the chair and the candle and the picture came down in a heap together. The candle went out.

"What on earth?" said Bill.

I felt the same. I picked up the candle and lit it, and then a most fearful thing happened. The old man picked himself up, and suddenly collapsed into a chair and began to cry like a child. Of course, I could see it was only the Artistic Temperament, but still, believe me, it was devilish unpleasant. I looked at old Bill. Old Bill looked at me. We shut the door quick, and after that we didn't know what to do. I saw Bill look at the sideboard, and I knew what he was looking for. But we had taken the siphon upstairs, and his ideas of first-aid stopped short at squirting soda-water. We just waited, and presently old Yeardsley switched off, sat up, and began talking with a rush.

"Clarence, my boy, I was tempted. It was that burglary at Dryden Park. It tempted me. It made it all so simple. I knew you would put it down to the same gang, Clarence, my boy. I——"

It seemed to dawn upon him at this point that Clarence was not among those present.

"Clarence?" he said hesitatingly.

"He's in bed," I said.

"In bed! Then he doesn't know? Even now—Young men, I throw myself on your mercy. Don't be hard on me. Listen." He grabbed at Bill, who sidestepped. "I can explain everything—everything."

He gave a gulp.

"You are not artists, you two young men, but I will try to make you understand, make you realise what this picture means to me. I was two years painting it. It is my child. I watched it grow. I loved it. It was part of my life. Nothing would have induced me to sell it. And then Clarence married, and in a mad moment I gave my treasure to him. You cannot understand, you two young men, what agonies I suffered. The thing was done. It was irrevocable. I saw how Clarence valued the picture. I knew that I could never bring myself to ask him for it back. And yet I was lost without it. What could I do? Till this evening I could see no hope. Then came this story of the theft of the Romney from a house quite close to this, and I saw my way. Clarence would never suspect. He would put the robbery down to the same band of criminals who stole the Romney. Once the idea had come, I could not drive it out. I fought against it, but to no avail. At last I yielded, and crept down here to carry out my plan. You found me." He grabbed again, at me this time, and got me by the arm. He had a grip like a lobster. "Young man," he said, "you would not betray me? You would not tell Clarence?"

I was feeling most frightfully sorry for the poor old chap by this time, don't you know, but I thought it would be kindest to give it him straight instead of breaking it by degrees.

"I won't say a word to Clarence, Mr. Yeardsley," I said. "I quite understand your feelings. The Artistic Temperament, and all that sort of thing. I mean—what? *I* know. But I'm afraid—Well, look!"

I went to the door and switched on the electric light, and there, staring him in the face, were the two empty frames. He stood goggling at them in silence. Then he gave a sort of wheezy grunt.

"The gang! The burglars! They *have* been here, and they have taken Clarence's picture!" He paused. "It might have been mine! My Venus!" he whispered It was getting most fearfully painful, you know, but he had to know the truth.

"I'm awfully sorry, you know," I said. "But it *was*."

He started, poor old chap.

"Eh? What do you mean?"

"They *did* take your Venus."

"But I have it here."

I shook my head.

"That's Clarence's 'Jocund Spring,'" I said.

He jumped at it and straightened it out.

"What! What are you talking about? Do you think I don't know my own picture—my child—my Venus. See! My own signature in the corner. Can you read, boy? Look: 'Matthew Yeardsley.' This is *my* picture!"

And—well, by Jove, it *was*, don't you know!

Well, we got him off to bed, him and his infernal Venus, and we settled down to take a steady look at the position of affairs. Bill said it was my fault for getting hold of the wrong picture, and I said it was Bill's fault for fetching me such a crack on the jaw that I couldn't be expected to see what I was getting hold of, and then there was a pretty massive silence for a bit.

"Reggie," said Bill at last, "how exactly do you feel about facing Clarence and Elizabeth at breakfast?"

"Old scout," I said. "I was thinking much the same myself."

"Reggie," said Bill, "I happen to know there's a milk-train leaving Midford at three-fifteen. It isn't what you'd call a flier. It gets to London at about half-past nine. Well—er—in the circumstances, how about it?"

CHAPTER - 8

THE AUNT AND THE SLUGGARD

Now that it's all over, I may as well admit that there was a time during the rather funny affair of Rockmetteller Todd when I thought that Jeeves was going to let me down. The man had the appearance of being baffled.

Jeeves is my man, you know. Officially he pulls in his weekly wages for pressing my clothes and all that sort of thing; but actually he's more like what the poet Johnnie called some bird of his acquaintance who was apt to rally round him in times of need—a guide, don't you know; philosopher, if I remember rightly, and—I rather fancy—friend. I rely on him at every turn.

So naturally, when Rocky Todd told me about his aunt, I didn't hesitate. Jeeves was in on the thing from the start.

The affair of Rocky Todd broke loose early one morning of spring. I was in bed, restoring the good old tissues with about nine hours of the dreamless, when the door flew open and somebody prodded me in the lower ribs and began to shake the bedclothes. After blinking a bit and generally pulling myself together, I located Rocky, and my first impression was that it was some horrid dream.

Rocky, you see, lived down on Long Island somewhere, miles away from New York; and not only that, but he had told me himself more than once that he never got up before twelve, and seldom earlier than one. Constitutionally the laziest young devil in America, he had hit on a walk in life which enabled him to go the limit in that direction. He was a poet. At least, he wrote poems when he did anything; but most of his time, as far as I could make out, he spent in a sort of trance. He told me once that he could sit on a fence, watching a worm and wondering what on earth it was up to, for hours at a stretch.

He had his scheme of life worked out to a fine point. About once a month he would take three days writing a few poems; the other three hundred and twenty-nine days of the year he rested. I didn't know there was enough money in poetry to support a chappie, even in the way in which Rocky lived; but it seems that, if you stick to exhortations to young men to lead the strenuous life and don't shove in any rhymes, American editors fight for the stuff. Rocky showed me one of his things once. It began:

Be!

Be!
The past is dead.
To-morrow is not born.
Be to-day!
To-day!
Be with every nerve,
With every muscle,
With every drop of your red blood!
Be!

It was printed opposite the frontispiece of a magazine with a sort of scroll round it, and a picture in the middle of a fairly-nude chappie, with bulging muscles, giving the rising sun the glad eye. Rocky said they gave him a hundred dollars for it, and he stayed in bed till four in the afternoon for over a month.

As regarded the future he was pretty solid, owing to the fact that he had a moneyed aunt tucked away somewhere in Illinois; and, as he had been named Rockmetteller after her, and was her only nephew, his position was pretty sound. He told me that when he did come into the money he meant to do no work at all, except perhaps an occasional poem recommending the young man with life opening out before him, with all its splendid possibilities, to light a pipe and shove his feet upon the mantelpiece.

And this was the man who was prodding me in the ribs in the grey dawn!

"Read this, Bertie!" I could just see that he was waving a letter or something equally foul in my face. "Wake up and read this!"

I can't read before I've had my morning tea and a cigarette. I groped for the bell.

Jeeves came in looking as fresh as a dewy violet. It's a mystery to me how he does it.

"Tea, Jeeves."

"Very good, sir."

He flowed silently out of the room—he always gives you the impression of being some liquid substance when he moves; and I found that Rocky was surging round with his beastly letter again.

"What is it?" I said. "What on earth's the matter?"

"Read it!"

"I can't. I haven't had my tea."

"Well, listen then."

"Who's it from?"

"My aunt."

At this point I fell asleep again. I woke to hear him saying:

"So what on earth am I to do?"

Jeeves trickled in with the tray, like some silent stream meandering over its mossy bed; and I saw daylight.

"Read it again, Rocky, old top," I said. "I want Jeeves to hear it. Mr. Todd's aunt has written him a rather rummy letter, Jeeves, and we want your advice."

"Very good, sir."

He stood in the middle of the room, registering devotion to the cause, and Rocky started again:

"MY DEAR ROCKMETTELLER.—I have been thinking things over for a long while, and I have come to the conclusion that I have been very thoughtless to wait so long before doing what I have made up my mind to do now."

"What do you make of that, Jeeves?"

"It seems a little obscure at present, sir, but no doubt it becomes cleared at a later point in the communication."

"It becomes as clear as mud!" said Rocky.

"Proceed, old scout," I said, champing my bread and butter.

"You know how all my life I have longed to visit New York and see for myself the wonderful gay life of which I have read so much. I fear that now it will be impossible for me to fulfil my dream. I am old and worn out. I seem to have no strength left in me."

"Sad, Jeeves, what?"

"Extremely, sir."

"Sad nothing!" said Rocky. "It's sheer laziness. I went to see her last Christmas and she was bursting with health. Her doctor told me himself that there was nothing wrong with her whatever. But she will insist that she's a hopeless invalid, so he has to agree with her. She's got a fixed idea that the trip to New York would kill her; so, though it's been her ambition all her life to come here, she stays where she is."

"Rather like the chappie whose heart was 'in the Highlands a-chasing of the deer,' Jeeves?"

"The cases are in some respects parallel, sir."

"Carry on, Rocky, dear boy."

"So I have decided that, if I cannot enjoy all the marvels of the city myself, I can at least enjoy them through you. I suddenly thought of this yesterday after reading a beautiful poem in the Sunday paper about a young man who had longed all his life for a certain thing and won it in the end only when he was too old to enjoy it. It was very sad, and it touched me."

"A thing," interpolated Rocky bitterly, "that I've not been able to do in ten years."

"As you know, you will have my money when I am gone; but until now I have never been able to see my way to giving you an allowance. I have now decided to do so—on one condition. I have written to a firm of lawyers in New

York, giving them instructions to pay you quite a substantial sum each month. My one condition is that you live in New York and enjoy yourself as I have always wished to do. I want you to be my representative, to spend this money for me as I should do myself. I want you to plunge into the gay, prismatic life of New York. I want you to be the life and soul of brilliant supper parties.

"Above all, I want you—indeed, I insist on this—to write me letters at least once a week giving me a full description of all you are doing and all that is going on in the city, so that I may enjoy at second-hand what my wretched health prevents my enjoying for myself. Remember that I shall expect full details, and that no detail is too trivial to interest.—Your affectionate Aunt,

"ISABEL ROCKMETTELLER."

"What about it?" said Rocky.

"What about it?" I said.

"Yes. What on earth am I going to do?"

It was only then that I really got on to the extremely rummy attitude of the chappie, in view of the fact that a quite unexpected mess of the right stuff had suddenly descended on him from a blue sky. To my mind it was an occasion for the beaming smile and the joyous whoop; yet here the man was, looking and talking as if Fate had swung on his solar plexus. It amazed me.

"Aren't you bucked?" I said.

"Bucked!"

"If I were in your place I should be frightfully braced. I consider this pretty soft for you."

He gave a kind of yelp, stared at me for a moment, and then began to talk of New York in a way that reminded me of Jimmy Mundy, the reformer chappie. Jimmy had just come to New York on a hit-the-trail campaign, and I had popped in at the Garden a couple of days before, for half an hour or so, to hear him. He had certainly told New York some pretty straight things about itself, having apparently taken a dislike to the place, but, by Jove, you know, dear old Rocky made him look like a publicity agent for the old metrop.!

"Pretty soft!" he cried. "To have to come and live in New York! To have to leave my little cottage and take a stuffy, smelly, over-heated hole of an apartment in this Heaven-forsaken, festering Gehenna. To have to mix night after night with a mob who think that life is a sort of St. Vitus's dance, and imagine that they're having a good time because they're making enough noise for six and drinking too much for ten. I loathe New York, Bertie. I wouldn't come near the place if I hadn't got to see editors occasionally. There's a blight on it. It's got moral delirium tremens. It's the limit. The very thought of staying more than a day in it makes me sick. And you call this thing pretty soft for me!"

I felt rather like Lot's friends must have done when they dropped in for a quiet chat and their genial host began to criticise the Cities of the Plain. I had no idea old Rocky could be so eloquent.

"It would kill me to have to live in New York," he went on. "To have to share the air with six million people! To have to wear stiff collars and decent clothes all the time! To——" He started. "Good Lord! I suppose I should have to dress for dinner in the evenings. What a ghastly notion!"

I was shocked, absolutely shocked.

"My dear chap!" I said reproachfully.

"Do you dress for dinner every night, Bertie?"

"Jeeves," I said coldly. The man was still standing like a statue by the door. "How many suits of evening clothes have I?"

"We have three suits full of evening dress, sir; two dinner jackets——"

"Three."

"For practical purposes two only, sir. If you remember we cannot wear the third. We have also seven white waistcoats."

"And shirts?"

"Four dozen, sir."

"And white ties?"

"The first two shallow shelves in the chest of drawers are completely filled with our white ties, sir."

I turned to Rocky.

"You see?"

The chappie writhed like an electric fan.

"I won't do it! I can't do it! I'll be hanged if I'll do it! How on earth can I dress up like that? Do you realize that most days I don't get out of my pyjamas till five in the afternoon, and then I just put on an old sweater?"

I saw Jeeves wince, poor chap! This sort of revelation shocked his finest feelings.

"Then, what are you going to do about it?" I said.

"That's what I want to know."

"You might write and explain to your aunt."

"I might—if I wanted her to get round to her lawyer's in two rapid leaps and cut me out of her will."

I saw his point.

"What do you suggest, Jeeves?" I said.

Jeeves cleared his throat respectfully.

"The crux of the matter would appear to be, sir, that Mr. Todd is obliged by the conditions under which the money is delivered into his possession to write Miss Rockmetteller long and detailed letters relating to his movements, and the only method by which this can be accomplished, if Mr. Todd adheres to his expressed intention of remaining in the country, is for Mr. Todd to induce some second party to gather the actual experiences which Miss Rockmetteller wishes reported to her, and to convey these to him in the shape of a careful report, on which it would be possible for him, with the aid of his imagination, to base the suggested correspondence."

Having got which off the old diaphragm, Jeeves was silent. Rocky looked at me in a helpless sort of way. He hasn't been brought up on Jeeves as I have, and he isn't on to his curves.

"Could he put it a little clearer, Bertie?" he said. "I thought at the start it was going to make sense, but it kind of flickered. What's the idea?"

"My dear old man, perfectly simple. I knew we could stand on Jeeves. All you've got to do is to get somebody to go round the town for you and take a few notes, and then you work the notes up into letters. That's it, isn't it, Jeeves?"

"Precisely, sir."

The light of hope gleamed in Rocky's eyes. He looked at Jeeves in a startled way, dazed by the man's vast intellect.

"But who would do it?" he said. "It would have to be a pretty smart sort of man, a man who would notice things."

"Jeeves!" I said. "Let Jeeves do it."

"But would he?"

"You would do it, wouldn't you, Jeeves?"

For the first time in our long connection I observed Jeeves almost smile. The corner of his mouth curved quite a quarter of an inch, and for a moment his eye ceased to look like a meditative fish's.

"I should be delighted to oblige, sir. As a matter of fact, I have already visited some of New York's places of interest on my evening out, and it would be most enjoyable to make a practice of the pursuit."

"Fine! I know exactly what your aunt wants to hear about, Rocky. She wants an earful of cabaret stuff. The place you ought to go to first, Jeeves, is Reigelheimer's. It's on Forty-second Street. Anybody will show you the way."

Jeeves shook his head.

"Pardon me, sir. People are no longer going to Reigelheimer's. The place at the moment is Frolics on the Roof."

"You see?" I said to Rocky. "Leave it to Jeeves. He knows."

It isn't often that you find an entire group of your fellow-humans happy in this world; but our little circle was certainly an example of the fact that it can be done. We were all full of beans. Everything went absolutely right from the start.

Jeeves was happy, partly because he loves to exercise his giant brain, and partly because he was having a corking time among the bright lights. I saw him one night at the Midnight Revels. He was sitting at a table on the edge of the dancing floor, doing himself remarkably well with a fat cigar and a bottle of the best. I'd never imagined he could look so nearly human. His face wore an expression of austere benevolence, and he was making notes in a small book.

As for the rest of us, I was feeling pretty good, because I was fond of old Rocky and glad to be able to do him a good turn. Rocky was perfectly contented, because he was still able to sit on fences in his pyjamas and watch worms. And, as for the aunt, she seemed tickled to death. She was getting Broadway at pretty long range, but it seemed to be hitting her just right. I read one of her letters to Rocky, and it was full of life.

But then Rocky's letters, based on Jeeves's notes, were enough to buck anybody up. It was rummy when you came to think of it. There was I, loving the life, while the mere mention of it gave Rocky a tired feeling; yet here is a letter I wrote to a pal of mine in London:

"DEAR FREDDIE,—Well, here I am in New York. It's not a bad place. I'm not having a bad time. Everything's pretty all right. The cabarets aren't bad. Don't know when I shall be back. How's everybody? Cheer-o!—Yours,

"BERTIE.

"PS.—Seen old Ted lately?"

Not that I cared about Ted; but if I hadn't dragged him in I couldn't have got the confounded thing on to the second page.

Now here's old Rocky on exactly the same subject:

"DEAREST AUNT ISABEL,—How can I ever thank you enough for giving me the opportunity to live in this astounding city! New York seems more wonderful every day.

"Fifth Avenue is at its best, of course, just now. The dresses are magnificent!"

Wads of stuff about the dresses. I didn't know Jeeves was such an authority.

"I was out with some of the crowd at the Midnight Revels the other night. We took in a show first, after a little dinner at a new place on Forty-third Street. We were quite a gay party. Georgie Cohan looked in about midnight and got off a good one about Willie Collier. Fred Stone could only stay a minute, but Doug. Fairbanks did all sorts of stunts and made us roar. Diamond Jim Brady was there, as usual, and Laurette Taylor showed up with a party. The show at the Revels is quite good. I am enclosing a programme.

"Last night a few of us went round to Frolics on the Roof——"

And so on and so forth, yards of it. I suppose it's the artistic temperament or something. What I mean is, it's easier for a chappie who's used to writing poems and that sort of tosh to put a bit of a punch into a letter than it is for a chappie like me. Anyway, there's no doubt that Rocky's correspondence was hot stuff. I called Jeeves in and congratulated him.

"Jeeves, you're a wonder!"

"Thank you, sir."

"How you notice everything at these places beats me. I couldn't tell you a thing about them, except that I've had a good time."

"It's just a knack, sir."

"Well, Mr. Todd's letters ought to brace Miss Rockmetteller all right, what?"

"Undoubtedly, sir," agreed Jeeves.

And, by Jove, they did! They certainly did, by George! What I mean to say is, I was sitting in the apartment one afternoon, about a month after the thing had started, smoking a cigarette and resting the old bean, when the door opened and the voice of Jeeves burst the silence like a bomb.

It wasn't that he spoke loud. He has one of those soft, soothing voices that slide through the atmosphere like the note of a far-off sheep. It was what he said made me leap like a young gazelle.

"Miss Rockmetteller!"

And in came a large, solid female.

The situation floored me. I'm not denying it. Hamlet must have felt much as I did when his father's ghost bobbed up in the fairway. I'd come to look on Rocky's aunt as such a permanency at her own home that it didn't seem possible that she could really be here in New York. I stared at her. Then I looked at Jeeves. He was standing there in an attitude of dignified detachment, the chump, when, if ever he should have been rallying round the young master, it was now.

Rocky's aunt looked less like an invalid than any one I've ever seen, except my Aunt Agatha. She had a good deal of Aunt Agatha about her, as a matter of fact. She looked as if she might be deucedly dangerous if put upon; and something seemed to tell me that she would certainly regard herself as put upon if she ever found out the game which poor old Rocky had been pulling on her.

"Good afternoon," I managed to say.

"How do you do?" she said. "Mr. Cohan?"

"Er—no."

"Mr. Fred Stone?"

"Not absolutely. As a matter of fact, my name's Wooster—Bertie Wooster."

She seemed disappointed. The fine old name of Wooster appeared to mean nothing in her life.

"Isn't Rockmetteller home?" she said. "Where is he?"

She had me with the first shot. I couldn't think of anything to say. I couldn't tell her that Rocky was down in the country, watching worms.

There was the faintest flutter of sound in the background. It was the respectful cough with which Jeeves announces that he is about to speak without having been spoken to.

"If you remember, sir, Mr. Todd went out in the automobile with a party in the afternoon."

"So he did, Jeeves; so he did," I said, looking at my watch. "Did he say when he would be back?"

"He gave me to understand, sir, that he would be somewhat late in returning."

He vanished; and the aunt took the chair which I'd forgotten to offer her. She looked at me in rather a rummy way. It was a nasty look. It made me feel as if I were something the dog had brought in and intended to bury later on, when he had time. My own Aunt Agatha, back in England, has looked at me in exactly the same way many a time, and it never fails to make my spine curl.

"You seem very much at home here, young man. Are you a great friend of Rockmetteller's?"

"Oh, yes, rather!"

She frowned as if she had expected better things of old Rocky.

"Well, you need to be," she said, "the way you treat his flat as your own!"

I give you my word, this quite unforeseen slam simply robbed me of the power of speech. I'd been looking on myself in the light of the dashing host, and suddenly to be treated as an intruder jarred me. It wasn't, mark you, as if she had spoken in a way to suggest that she considered my presence in the place as an ordinary social call. She obviously looked on me as a cross between a burglar and the plumber's man come to fix the leak in the bathroom. It hurt her—my being there.

At this juncture, with the conversation showing every sign of being about to die in awful agonies, an idea came to me. Tea—the good old stand-by.

"Would you care for a cup of tea?" I said.

"Tea?"

She spoke as if she had never heard of the stuff.

"Nothing like a cup after a journey," I said. "Bucks you up! Puts a bit of zip into you. What I mean is, restores you, and so on, don't you know. I'll go and tell Jeeves."

I tottered down the passage to Jeeves's lair. The man was reading the evening paper as if he hadn't a care in the world.

"Jeeves," I said, "we want some tea."

"Very good, sir."

"I say, Jeeves, this is a bit thick, what?"

I wanted sympathy, don't you know—sympathy and kindness. The old nerve centres had had the deuce of a shock.

"She's got the idea this place belongs to Mr. Todd. What on earth put that into her head?"

Jeeves filled the kettle with a restrained dignity.

"No doubt because of Mr. Todd's letters, sir," he said. "It was my suggestion, sir, if you remember, that they should be addressed from this apartment in order that Mr. Todd should appear to possess a good central residence in the city."

I remembered. We had thought it a brainy scheme at the time.

"Well, it's bally awkward, you know, Jeeves. She looks on me as an intruder.

By Jove! I suppose she thinks I'm someone who hangs about here, touching Mr. Todd for free meals and borrowing his shirts."

"Yes, sir."

"It's pretty rotten, you know."

"Most disturbing, sir."

"And there's another thing: What are we to do about Mr. Todd? We've got to get him up here as soon as ever we can. When you have brought the tea you had better go out and send him a telegram, telling him to come up by the next train."

"I have already done so, sir. I took the liberty of writing the message and dispatching it by the lift attendant."

"By Jove, you think of everything, Jeeves!"

"Thank you, sir. A little buttered toast with the tea? Just so, sir. Thank you."

I went back to the sitting-room. She hadn't moved an inch. She was still bolt upright on the edge of her chair, gripping her umbrella like a hammer-thrower. She gave me another of those looks as I came in. There was no doubt about it; for some reason she had taken a dislike to me. I suppose because I wasn't George M. Cohan. It was a bit hard on a chap.

"This is a surprise, what?" I said, after about five minutes' restful silence, trying to crank the conversation up again.

"What is a surprise?"

"Your coming here, don't you know, and so on."

She raised her eyebrows and drank me in a bit more through her glasses.

"Why is it surprising that I should visit my only nephew?" she said.

Put like that, of course, it did seem reasonable.

"Oh, rather," I said. "Of course! Certainly. What I mean is——"

Jeeves projected himself into the room with the tea. I was jolly glad to see him. There's nothing like having a bit of business arranged for one when one isn't certain of one's lines. With the teapot to fool about with I felt happier.

"Tea, tea, tea—what? What?" I said.

It wasn't what I had meant to say. My idea had been to be a good deal more formal, and so on. Still, it covered the situation. I poured her out a cup. She sipped it and put the cup down with a shudder.

"Do you mean to say, young man," she said frostily, "that you expect me to drink this stuff?"

"Rather! Bucks you up, you know."

"What do you mean by the expression 'Bucks you up'?"

"Well, makes you full of beans, you know. Makes you fizz."

"I don't understand a word you say. You're English, aren't you?"

I admitted it. She didn't say a word. And somehow she did it in a way that made it worse than if she had spoken for hours. Somehow it was brought home to me that she didn't like Englishmen, and that if she had had to meet an Englishman, I was the one she'd have chosen last.

Conversation languished again after that.

Then I tried again. I was becoming more convinced every moment that you can't make a real lively *salon* with a couple of people, especially if one of them lets it go a word at a time.

"Are you comfortable at your hotel?" I said.

"At which hotel?"

"The hotel you're staying at."

"I am not staying at an hotel."

"Stopping with friends—what?"

"I am naturally stopping with my nephew."

I didn't get it for the moment; then it hit me.

"What! Here?" I gurgled.

"Certainly! Where else should I go?"

The full horror of the situation rolled over me like a wave. I couldn't see what on earth I was to do. I couldn't explain that this wasn't Rocky's flat without giving the poor old chap away hopelessly, because she would then ask me where he did live, and then he would be right in the soup. I was trying to induce the old bean to recover from the shock and produce some results when she spoke again.

"Will you kindly tell my nephew's man-servant to prepare my room? I wish to lie down."

"Your nephew's man-servant?"

"The man you call Jeeves. If Rockmetteller has gone for an automobile ride, there is no need for you to wait for him. He will naturally wish to be alone with me when he returns."

I found myself tottering out of the room. The thing was too much for me. I crept into Jeeves's den.

"Jeeves!" I whispered.

"Sir?"

"Mix me a b.-and-s., Jeeves. I feel weak."

"Very good, sir."

"This is getting thicker every minute, Jeeves."

"Sir?"

"She thinks you're Mr. Todd's man. She thinks the whole place is his, and everything in it. I don't see what you're to do, except stay on and keep it up. We can't say anything or she'll get on to the whole thing, and I don't want to let Mr. Todd down. By the way, Jeeves, she wants you to prepare her bed."

He looked wounded.

"It is hardly my place, sir——"

"I know—I know. But do it as a personal favour to me. If you come to that, it's hardly my place to be flung out of the flat like this and have to go to an hotel, what?"

"Is it your intention to go to an hotel, sir? What will you do for clothes?"

"Good Lord! I hadn't thought of that. Can you put a few things in a bag when she isn't looking, and sneak them down to me at the St. Aurea?"

"I will endeavour to do so, sir."

"Well, I don't think there's anything more, is there? Tell Mr. Todd where I am when he gets here."

"Very good, sir."

I looked round the place. The moment of parting had come. I felt sad. The whole thing reminded me of one of those melodramas where they drive chappies out of the old homestead into the snow.

"Good-bye, Jeeves," I said.

"Good-bye, sir."

And I staggered out.

You know, I rather think I agree with those poet-and-philosopher Johnnies who insist that a fellow ought to be devilish pleased if he has a bit of trouble. All that stuff about being refined by suffering, you know. Suffering does give a chap a sort of broader and more sympathetic outlook. It helps you to understand other people's misfortunes if you've been through the same thing yourself.

As I stood in my lonely bedroom at the hotel, trying to tie my white tie myself, it struck me for the first time that there must be whole squads of chappies in the world who had to get along without a man to look after them. I'd always thought of Jeeves as a kind of natural phenomenon; but, by Jove! of course, when you come to think of it, there must be quite a lot of fellows who have to press their own clothes themselves and haven't got anybody to bring them tea in the morning, and so on. It was rather a solemn thought, don't you know. I mean to say, ever since then I've been able to appreciate the frightful privations the poor have to stick.

I got dressed somehow. Jeeves hadn't forgotten a thing in his packing. Everything was there, down to the final stud. I'm not sure this didn't make me feel worse. It kind of deepened the pathos. It was like what somebody or other wrote about the touch of a vanished hand.

I had a bit of dinner somewhere and went to a show of some kind; but nothing seemed to make any difference. I simply hadn't the heart to go on to supper anywhere. I just sucked down a whisky-and-soda in the hotel smoking-room and went straight up to bed. I don't know when I've felt so rotten. Somehow I found myself moving about the room softly, as if there had been a death in the family. If I had anybody to talk to I should have talked in a whisper;

in fact, when the telephone-bell rang I answered in such a sad, hushed voice that the fellow at the other end of the wire said "Halloa!" five times, thinking he hadn't got me.

It was Rocky. The poor old scout was deeply agitated.

"Bertie! Is that you, Bertie! Oh, gosh? I'm having a time!"

"Where are you speaking from?"

"The Midnight Revels. We've been here an hour, and I think we're a fixture for the night. I've told Aunt Isabel I've gone out to call up a friend to join us. She's glued to a chair, with this-is-the-life written all over her, taking it in through the pores. She loves it, and I'm nearly crazy."

"Tell me all, old top," I said.

"A little more of this," he said, "and I shall sneak quietly off to the river and end it all. Do you mean to say you go through this sort of thing every night, Bertie, and enjoy it? It's simply infernal! I was just snatching a wink of sleep behind the bill of fare just now when about a million yelling girls swooped down, with toy balloons. There are two orchestras here, each trying to see if it can't play louder than the other. I'm a mental and physical wreck. When your telegram arrived I was just lying down for a quiet pipe, with a sense of absolute peace stealing over me. I had to get dressed and sprint two miles to catch the train. It nearly gave me heart-failure; and on top of that I almost got brain fever inventing lies to tell Aunt Isabel. And then I had to cram myself into these confounded evening clothes of yours."

I gave a sharp wail of agony. It hadn't struck me till then that Rocky was depending on my wardrobe to see him through.

"You'll ruin them!"

"I hope so," said Rocky, in the most unpleasant way. His troubles seemed to have had the worst effect on his character. "I should like to get back at them somehow; they've given me a bad enough time. They're about three sizes too small, and something's apt to give at any moment. I wish to goodness it would, and give me a chance to breathe. I haven't breathed since half-past seven. Thank Heaven, Jeeves managed to get out and buy me a collar that fitted, or I should be a strangled corpse by now! It was touch and go till the stud broke. Bertie, this is pure Hades! Aunt Isabel keeps on urging me to dance. How on earth can I dance when I don't know a soul to dance with? And how the deuce could I, even if I knew every girl in the place? It's taking big chances even to move in these trousers. I had to tell her I've hurt my ankle. She keeps asking me when Cohan and Stone are going to turn up; and it's simply a question of time before she discovers that Stone is sitting two tables away. Something's got to be done, Bertie! You've got to think up some way of getting me out of this mess. It was you who got me into it."

"Me! What do you mean?"

"Well, Jeeves, then. It's all the same. It was you who suggested leaving it to Jeeves. It was those letters I wrote from his notes that did the mischief. I made them too good! My aunt's just been telling me about it. She says she had resigned herself to ending her life where she was, and then my letters began to arrive, describing the joys of New York; and they stimulated her to such an extent that she pulled herself together and made the trip. She seems to think she's had some miraculous kind of faith cure. I tell you I can't stand it, Bertie! It's got to end!"

"Can't Jeeves think of anything?"

"No. He just hangs round saying: 'Most disturbing, sir!' A fat lot of help that is!"

"Well, old lad," I said, "after all, it's far worse for me than it is for you. You've got a comfortable home and Jeeves. And you're saving a lot of money."

"Saving money? What do you mean—saving money?"

"Why, the allowance your aunt was giving you. I suppose she's paying all the expenses now, isn't she?"

"Certainly she is; but she's stopped the allowance. She wrote the lawyers to-night. She says that, now she's in New York, there is no necessity for it to go on, as we shall always be together, and it's simpler for her to look after that end of it. I tell you, Bertie, I've examined the darned cloud with a microscope, and if it's got a silver lining it's some little dissembler!"

"But, Rocky, old top, it's too bally awful! You've no notion of what I'm going through in this beastly hotel, without Jeeves. I must get back to the flat."

"Don't come near the flat."

"But it's my own flat."

"I can't help that. Aunt Isabel doesn't like you. She asked me what you did for a living. And when I told her you didn't do anything she said she thought as much, and that you were a typical specimen of a useless and decaying aristocracy. So if you think you have made a hit, forget it. Now I must be going back, or she'll be coming out here after me. Good-bye."

Next morning Jeeves came round. It was all so home-like when he floated noiselessly into the room that I nearly broke down.

"Good morning, sir," he said. "I have brought a few more of your personal belongings."

He began to unstrap the suit-case he was carrying.

"Did you have any trouble sneaking them away?"

"It was not easy, sir. I had to watch my chance. Miss Rockmetteller is a remarkably alert lady."

"You know, Jeeves, say what you like—this is a bit thick, isn't it?"

"The situation is certainly one that has never before come under my notice, sir. I have brought the heather-mixture suit, as the climatic conditions are congenial. To-morrow, if not prevented, I will endeavour to add the brown lounge with the faint green twill."

"It can't go on—this sort of thing—Jeeves."

"We must hope for the best, sir."

"Can't you think of anything to do?"

"I have been giving the matter considerable thought, sir, but so far without success. I am placing three silk shirts—the dove-coloured, the light blue, and the mauve—in the first long drawer, sir."

"You don't mean to say you can't think of anything, Jeeves?"

"For the moment, sir, no. You will find a dozen handkerchiefs and the tan socks in the upper drawer on the left." He strapped the suit-case and put it on a chair. "A curious lady, Miss Rockmetteller, sir."

"You understate it, Jeeves."

He gazed meditatively out of the window.

"In many ways, sir, Miss Rockmetteller reminds me of an aunt of mine who resides in the south-east portion of London. Their temperaments are much alike. My aunt has the same taste for the pleasures of the great city. It is a passion with her to ride in hansom cabs, sir. Whenever the family take their eyes off her she escapes from the house and spends the day riding about in cabs. On several occasions she has broken into the children's savings bank to secure the means to enable her to gratify this desire."

"I love to have these little chats with you about your female relatives, Jeeves," I said coldly, for I felt that the man had let me down, and I was fed up with him. "But I don't see what all this has got to do with my trouble."

"I beg your pardon, sir. I am leaving a small assortment of neckties on the mantelpiece, sir, for you to select according to your preference. I should recommend the blue with the red domino pattern, sir."

Then he streamed imperceptibly toward the door and flowed silently out.

I've often heard that chappies, after some great shock or loss, have a habit, after they've been on the floor for a while wondering what hit them, of picking themselves up and piecing themselves together, and sort of taking a whirl at beginning a new life. Time, the great healer, and Nature, adjusting itself, and so on and so forth. There's a lot in it. I know, because in my own case, after a day or two of what you might call prostration, I began to recover. The frightful loss of Jeeves made any thought of pleasure more or less a mockery, but at least I found that I was able to have a dash at enjoying life again. What I mean is, I was braced up to the extent of going round the cabarets once more, so as to try to forget, if only for the moment.

New York's a small place when it comes to the part of it that wakes up just as the rest is going to bed, and it wasn't long before my tracks began to cross old Rocky's. I saw him once at Peale's, and again at Frolics on the roof. There wasn't anybody with him either time except the aunt, and, though he was trying to look as if he had struck the ideal life, it wasn't difficult for me, knowing the circumstances, to see that beneath the mask the poor chap was suffering. My heart bled for the fellow. At least, what there was of it that wasn't bleeding for myself bled for him. He had the air of one who was about to crack under the strain.

It seemed to me that the aunt was looking slightly upset also. I took it that she was beginning to wonder when the celebrities were going to surge round, and what had suddenly become of all those wild, careless spirits Rocky used to mix with in his letters. I didn't blame her. I had only read a couple of his letters, but they certainly gave the impression that poor old Rocky was by way of being the hub of New York night life, and that, if by any chance he failed to show up at a cabaret, the management said: "What's the use?" and put up the shutters.

The next two nights I didn't come across them, but the night after that I was sitting by myself at the Maison Pierre when somebody tapped me on the shoulder-blade, and I found Rocky standing beside me, with a sort of mixed expression of wistfulness and apoplexy on his face. How the chappie had contrived to wear my evening clothes so many times without disaster was a mystery to me. He confided later that early in the proceedings he had slit the waistcoat up the back and that that had helped a bit.

For a moment I had the idea that he had managed to get away from his aunt for the evening; but, looking past him, I saw that she was in again. She was at a table over by the wall, looking at me as if I were something the management ought to be complained to about.

"Bertie, old scout," said Rocky, in a quiet, sort of crushed voice, "we've always been pals, haven't we? I mean, you know I'd do you a good turn if you asked me?"

"My dear old lad," I said. The man had moved me.

"Then, for Heaven's sake, come over and sit at our table for the rest of the evening."

Well, you know, there are limits to the sacred claims of friendship.

"My dear chap," I said, "you know I'd do anything in reason; but——"

"You must come, Bertie. You've got to. Something's got to be done to divert her mind. She's brooding about something. She's been like that for the last two days. I think she's beginning to suspect. She can't understand why we never seem to meet anyone I know at these joints. A few nights ago I happened to run into two newspaper men I used to know fairly well. That kept me going for a while. I introduced them to Aunt Isabel as David Belasco and Jim Corbett, and it went well. But the effect has worn off now, and she's beginning to wonder again. Something's got to be done, or she will find out everything, and if she does I'd take a nickel for my chance of getting a cent from her later on. So, for the love of Mike, come across to our table and help things along."

I went along. One has to rally round a pal in distress. Aunt Isabel was sitting bolt upright, as usual. It certainly did seem as if she had lost a bit of the zest with which she had started out to explore Broadway. She looked as if she had been thinking a good deal about rather unpleasant things.

"You've met Bertie Wooster, Aunt Isabel?" said Rocky.

"I have."

There was something in her eye that seemed to say:

"Out of a city of six million people, why did you pick on me?"

"Take a seat, Bertie. What'll you have?" said Rocky.

And so the merry party began. It was one of those jolly, happy, bread-crumbling parties where you cough twice before you speak, and then decide not to say it after all. After we had had an hour of this wild dissipation, Aunt Isabel said she wanted to go home. In the light of what Rocky had been telling me, this struck me as sinister. I had gathered that at the beginning of her visit she had had to be dragged home with ropes.

It must have hit Rocky the same way, for he gave me a pleading look.

"You'll come along, won't you, Bertie, and have a drink at the flat?"

I had a feeling that this wasn't in the contract, but there wasn't anything to be done. It seemed brutal to leave the poor chap alone with the woman, so I went along.

Right from the start, from the moment we stepped into the taxi, the feeling began to grow that something was about to break loose. A massive silence prevailed in the corner where the aunt sat, and, though Rocky, balancing himself on the little seat in front, did his best to supply dialogue, we weren't a chatty party.

I had a glimpse of Jeeves as we went into the flat, sitting in his lair, and I wished I could have called to him to rally round. Something told me that I was about to need him.

The stuff was on the table in the sitting-room. Rocky took up the decanter.

"Say when, Bertie."

"Stop!" barked the aunt, and he dropped it.

I caught Rocky's eye as he stooped to pick up the ruins. It was the eye of one who sees it coming.

"Leave it there, Rockmetteller!" said Aunt Isabel; and Rocky left it there.

"The time has come to speak," she said. "I cannot stand idly by and see a young man going to perdition!"

Poor old Rocky gave a sort of gurgle, a kind of sound rather like the whisky had made running out of the decanter on to my carpet.

"Eh?" he said, blinking.

The aunt proceeded.

"The fault," she said, "was mine. I had not then seen the light. But now my eyes are open. I see the hideous mistake I have made. I shudder at the thought of the wrong I did you, Rockmetteller, by urging you into contact with this wicked city."

I saw Rocky grope feebly for the table. His fingers touched it, and a look of relief came into the poor chappie's face. I understood his feelings.

"But when I wrote you that letter, Rockmetteller, instructing you to go to the city and live its life, I had not had the privilege of hearing Mr. Mundy speak on the subject of New York."

"Jimmy Mundy!" I cried.

You know how it is sometimes when everything seems all mixed up and you suddenly get a clue. When she mentioned Jimmy Mundy I began to understand more or less what had happened. I'd seen it happen before. I remember, back in England, the man I had before Jeeves sneaked off to a meeting on his evening out and came back and denounced me in front of a crowd of chappies I was giving a bit of supper to as a moral leper.

The aunt gave me a withering up and down.

"Yes; Jimmy Mundy!" she said. "I am surprised at a man of your stamp having heard of him. There is no music, there are no drunken, dancing men, no shameless, flaunting women at his meetings; so for you they would have no attraction. But for others, less dead in sin, he has his message. He has come to save New York from itself; to force it—in his picturesque phrase—to hit the trail. It was three days ago, Rockmetteller, that I first heard him. It was an accident that took me to his meeting. How often in this life a mere accident may shape our whole future!

"You had been called away by that telephone message from Mr. Belasco; so you could not take me to the Hippodrome, as we had arranged. I asked your man-servant, Jeeves, to take me there. The man has very little intelligence. He seems to have misunderstood me. I am thankful that he did. He took me to what I subsequently learned was Madison Square Garden, where Mr. Mundy is holding his meetings. He escorted me to a seat and then left me. And it was not till the meeting had begun that I discovered the mistake which had been made. My seat was in the middle of a row. I could not leave without inconveniencing a great many people, so I remained."

She gulped.

"Rockmetteller, I have never been so thankful for anything else. Mr. Mundy was wonderful! He was like some prophet of old, scourging the sins of the people. He leaped about in a frenzy of inspiration till I feared he would do himself an injury. Sometimes he expressed himself in a somewhat odd manner, but every word carried conviction. He showed me New York in its true colours. He showed me the vanity and wickedness of sitting in gilded haunts of vice, eating lobster when decent people should be in bed.

"He said that the tango and the fox-trot were devices of the devil to drag people down into the Bottomless Pit. He said that there was more sin in ten minutes with a negro banjo orchestra than in all the ancient revels of Nineveh and Babylon. And when he stood on one leg and pointed right at where I was sitting and shouted, 'This means you!' I could have sunk through the floor. I came away a changed woman. Surely you must have noticed the change in me, Rockmetteller? You must have seen that I was no longer the careless, thoughtless person who had urged you to dance in those places of wickedness?"

Rocky was holding on to the table as if it was his only friend.

"Y-yes," he stammered; "I—I thought something was wrong."

"Wrong? Something was right! Everything was right! Rockmetteller, it is not too late for you to be saved. You have only sipped of the evil cup. You have not drained it. It will be hard at first, but you will find that you can do it if you fight with a stout heart against the glamour and fascination of this dreadful city. Won't you, for my sake, try, Rockmetteller? Won't you go back to the country to-morrow and begin the struggle? Little by little, if you use your will——"

I can't help thinking it must have been that word "will" that roused dear old Rocky like a trumpet call. It must have brought home to him the realisation that a miracle had come off and saved him from being cut out of Aunt Isabel's. At any rate, as she said it he perked up, let go of the table, and faced her with gleaming eyes.

"Do you want me to go back to the country, Aunt Isabel?"

"Yes."

"Not to live in the country?"

"Yes, Rockmetteller."

"Stay in the country all the time, do you mean? Never come to New York?"

"Yes, Rockmetteller; I mean just that. It is the only way. Only there can you be safe from temptation. Will you do it, Rockmetteller? Will you—for my sake?"

Rocky grabbed the table again. He seemed to draw a lot of encouragement from that table.

"I will!" he said.

"Jeeves," I said. It was next day, and I was back in the old flat, lying in the old arm-chair, with my feet upon the good old table. I had just come from seeing dear old Rocky off to his country cottage, and an hour before he had seen his aunt off to whatever hamlet it was that she was the curse of; so we were alone at last. "Jeeves, there's no place like home—what?"

"Very true, sir."

"The jolly old roof-tree, and all that sort of thing—what?"

"Precisely, sir."

I lit another cigarette.

"Jeeves."

"Sir?"

"Do you know, at one point in the business I really thought you were baffled."

"Indeed, sir?"

"When did you get the idea of taking Miss Rockmetteller to the meeting? It was pure genius!"

"Thank you, sir. It came to me a little suddenly, one morning when I was thinking of my aunt, sir."

"Your aunt? The hansom cab one?"

"Yes, sir. I recollected that, whenever we observed one of her attacks coming on, we used to send for the clergyman of the parish. We always found that if he talked to her a while of higher things it diverted her mind from hansom cabs. It occurred to me that the same treatment might prove efficacious in the case of Miss Rockmetteller."

I was stunned by the man's resource.

"It's brain," I said; "pure brain! What do you do to get like that, Jeeves? I believe you must eat a lot of fish, or something. Do you eat a lot of fish, Jeeves?"

"No, sir."

"Oh, well, then, it's just a gift, I take it; and if you aren't born that way there's no use worrying."

"Precisely, sir," said Jeeves. "If I might make the suggestion, sir, I should not continue to wear your present tie. The green shade gives you a slightly bilious air. I should strongly advocate the blue with the red domino pattern instead, sir."

"All right, Jeeves." I said humbly. "You know!"

THE END